MENDING
FENCES
with the billionaire

Other Books By Lorin Grace

American Homespun Series
Waking Lucy
Remembering Anna
Reforming Elizabeth
Healing Sarah

Artists & Billionaires
Mending Christmas
Mending Walls
Mending Images
Mending Words
Mending Hearts

Artists & Billionaires 1

MENDING FENCES
with the billionaire

LORIN GRACE

CURRANT
CREEK PRESS

Cover Design © 2018 LJP Creative
Photos © iStock, Deposit Photos

Formatting by LJP Creative
Edits by Eschler Editing

Published by Currant Creek Press
North Logan, Utah

Second edition: August 2018
ISBN: 978-0-9984110-6-4

For Anita

one

ALL MANDY NEEDED WAS FOUR more inches to get the perfect shot, but no matter which direction she moved along the gate, the black-walnut tree blocked part of her view. She glanced over her shoulder. The only vehicle on the neglected lane was her ancient blue VW Golf, or the "Golf Ball," named for the many dents inflicted by an Indiana hailstorm. Vehicles sped by on the county road beyond. Still, she felt as if someone were watching her.

Sometime in the last decade, the old wrought-iron gate had been replaced with a standard metal five-row pole gate. The rock columns that supported the archway now crumbled from their lofty height to little taller than her own five and a half feet. Haphazard piles of rubble lay within the fence line—a victim of the tornado that had hopscotched across the area three years ago. New chain-link fencing replaced the old pole fence.

Mandy tested the gate. The chain didn't swing more than five inches either way. Climbing on the lowest rail and leaning over the top, she tried again, but the tree still obscured her view. The second rail wasn't any better, nor the third. On the fourth, her positioning became precarious but gave her the best view so far. After checking to make sure no one was watching, she swung her leg over the top rail and straddled the gate, adjusting her flowing skirt to keep the fabric from tangling around her knees. Grandma Mae's voice echoed in her head: *Amanda, ladies don't climb in dresses*," but she needed to take the shot. Not as clean a shot as she would get from inside the gate, but good enough. Mandy leaned as far as she dared to the right and focused through the viewfinder. Click.

"Hey! No trespassing!" a harsh male voice bellowed behind her.

Mandy turned to see who, and her world turned upside down. Her foot hit the ground first, but she kept going.

As the air came back into her lungs, three things came to her—the pain in her left foot, the blue, plastic-looking gun pointed at her face, and the portion of her skirt waving at her from the gate. Ignoring the toy gun, she sat up and yelped. There would be bruises. She tugged the remains of her skirt down. A chunk was missing from the right side, exposing more of her thigh than she was comfortable with.

The camera. Where was it? Several black lumps lay four feet away. She closed her eyes, hoping she was seeing double. No use. The camera lens lay in three pieces on the cracked asphalt. If she were lucky, the man holding the funny plastic gun would shoot her, and maybe it would fire real bullets and not water. Death would be better than facing her faculty adviser. She turned her attention to the gun holder.

"Can't you read?" He waved the gun toward one of the "No Trespassing" signs hanging every ten yards along the fence.

"Of course, I can. I was on that side of the fence. I am only trespassing because I fell." She attempted to look him in the eye, but the sun peeking at her over his shoulder forced her to squint.

"Get up."

Standing up in a skirt from her position was no easy feat. *Grandma Mae would have a hissy fit if she saw me now.*

"Hurry up."

"You can be a gentleman and put the gun away and give me a hand, or you can wait."

He chose to wait.

Mandy suppressed a cry as she stood, then adjusted her weight to her right leg.

"So, what were you doing? Coming to vandalize the old Crawford place?" Even standing she couldn't see his face well. The shadow of the hat he wore hid most of it.

"I think it should be fairly obvious my intention isn't to vandalize anything." Mandy pointed to the broken camera.

"You were climbing over the gate."

"I climbed *on* the gate. I had no intention of setting foot on the ground."

"Who sent you?" He waved the gun again.

Mandy gritted her teeth to keep the sarcastic comments inside. "No one sent me."

"That is what the last one said before hightailing it off to the land developers in Chicago."

Mandy hopped a step to the gate.

"Hold it right there."

She rolled her eyes. "Will you please put the squirt gun away so we can sort this out?"

The man shifted. He was younger than she'd first thought, only a year or two older than her twenty-six years.

She hopped again. "I know you don't believe me, but in case you haven't noticed, I am hardly in a position to run away or to hurt you."

He lowered the gun. "This isn't a squirt gun; it is the newest prototype of printable gun."

"That thing can shoot real bullets?" The thought that the plastic gun didn't squirt water caused a tremor to pass through her.

"It can, but in this case they are rubber." He slid the gun into a holster at his back.

Mandy hopped another step. "If you can give me a hand, I will leave. I seem to have injured my foot."

The man shook his head and walked over to the end of the gate, inserted a key in the padlock, and removed the chain. Instead of coming to help her, he walked over to the remains of the camera. "That looks like one expensive camera."

Mandy limped, using the gate for support. "Tell me about it."

"What did you say?" The man picked up the pieces and strode over to intercept her.

"I was agreeing. It is a very expensive camera."

Cradling the camera pieces, he blocked her way. "Probably more than a teenager like you can afford. Who paid you to come here?"

"Can't you read? The camera is clearly marked 'University Property.'" Mandy jabbed a finger at the UPC inventory sticker.

"Why would the university want pictures of this place?"

"They don't. I do. I borrowed the camera for my MFA project, and I'm not a teenager."

For a split second, Mandy thought she saw a flicker of something other than anger, but it was difficult to tell with the brim of his hat shading his face.

"You're bleeding." He pointed to her arm.

Blood trickled from her elbow. "Just a bit." Not like a few drops of blood were her biggest problem at the moment.

"Aren't you going to do something about that?"

"Like what? Rip the rest of my skirt off and wrap it?"

The man walked around her and retrieved the portion of her skirt still clinging to the upper rail. "Here."

"Thanks." His chivalry was unparalleled. She wrapped the remnant around her arm. He stood close enough now that she could see him clearly. She would know those blue eyes anywhere. "Danny?"

He stepped back. "No one calls me that. I don't care what you think you know from the tabloids. You don't know me."

"Yes, I do. The summer you lived here—"

"Stop." He shoved the camera and lens parts at her. "Just leave." He pushed the gate open wide.

Mandy felt him watching as she dumped the pieces in the camera bag she'd left on the side of the road. "And to think Grandma Mae thought you would grow up to be a gentleman," she muttered as she hoisted the bag to her shoulder. She winced when the strap hit a bruise.

Daniel froze in place, his hand on the gate. "What did you say?"

"I said Grandma Mae was wrong about you." Mandy limped to the car, the tears she had managed to keep at bay now escaping. She wasn't going to give him the satisfaction of seeing her cry. The old Danny would have helped her.

When she checked the rearview mirror, he still stood at the gate.

two

As the Golf disappeared in a cloud of dust, Daniel went inside the gate before locking it. Memories of the one summer he was allowed to be a child poured back as fast as he had downed Grandma Mae's lemonade.

How had he not recognized Amanda Fowler? The last photo he had seen of her had been from her high school graduation invitation sent by Grandma Mae, which he had ignored like all the Christmas cards that had stopped coming a while ago. She hadn't changed much since the photo was taken. Her hair might have been longer—hard to tell with it up in a ponytail—but it was still the soft-brown color of the deer they used to watch. And those eyes sparkled as vibrantly as they had twenty years ago. She had been wearing a skirt rather than cutoff jeans and the twigs she'd once had for legs…better not even go there.

He pulled out his phone and punched speed dial. "Hey, Colin, do me a favor. Flag the local hospital and emergency clinics for a Mandy, or Amanda Fowler? Then make sure the bill is paid in full."

The voice on the end of the line grunted. "You know how hard that is with HIPAA."

"Not as hard as you tell me it is." Colin had been his roommate from the time they were both ten years old at the boarding school they'd both detested until college, when they'd chosen different paths. Top of his class at MIT, Colin could probably get into any computer in the United States if he wanted to. Good thing they were still friends as well as business partners, like their fathers.

"Are you at the Indiana property?"

Daniel shifted his phone to the other ear. "Yes. I still can't decide what to do with it. I love the pond and the hills and all the trees, but Grandfather's monstrosity of a house, not so much. And before you ask, she hurt her ankle, and, no, I didn't touch her. She had an accident that was kind of my fault."

"Do I need to give legal a heads-up?"

"No, this one won't sue."

"Are you sure?"

Daniel stopped at the front door of the caretaker's house and punched in his code on the security pad. "I bet she doesn't even hit social media with the tale."

Colin laughed. "You're kidding. Is she eighty?"

"No, she turned twenty-six on February 9."

"Woah, there, how well do you know this woman?"

"Not the way you are thinking, Colin. Don't even go there."

"How do you know Miss She-Won't-Tell?" Colin's curiosity was annoying but justified. Over the last few months, every time Daniel even blinked at a woman, she tried to turn the gesture into some scandal to have her fifteen minutes of fame with one of America's most eligible bachelors, as determined by some group of publicists trying to sell magazines.

"Well, enough to know she was raised better than that." *Better than me.*

"That is no guarantee." Daniel heard Colin's rapid typing on the keyboard. No doubt he had flagged every one of Mandy Fowler's social media accounts. "I need better than that."

"She called me Danny."

Silence reverberated from the other end of the line. Daniel's thumb hovered above disconnect when Colin's voice came back on. "She checked into the county hospital ER. She is the little girl you used to talk about, isn't she?"

Not little anymore, but just as cute. "Colin, get the bill paid."

"Done."

"And, Colin. Stay out of the rest of her files. Anything not in the public eye stays out of yours. Got it?"

"Sure." Colin paused for a second. "If this is the Mandy I think it is, think before you act."

Too late for that.

Candace came rushing into the emergency room. "Mandy! How dare you send a text like that." Several heads turned toward her voice.

Mandy leaned forward and tried to shush her roommate. "People are looking."

"Let 'em look." But Mandy's roommate lowered her voice and took the molded plastic seat next to her.

Mandy rolled her eyes. "You say that because you like them looking."

Today Candace sported an oversized black art-deco T-shirt and vibrant blue-and-violet hair, one of her favorite wigs. She turned to a gawking toddler and smiled. The child laughed and pointed. "Look! Clown!" His mother picked him up and moved to the other side of the room.

Candace turned back to Mandy. "So, what happened? 'Fell at C Mansion. Meet at ER. DC is a jerk' is hardly enough information."

"I went to take a photo, and the—"

"Excuse me, Mandy Fowler?" A nurse parked a wheelchair in front of the two women. Mandy moved to the chair and jerked her head so Candace would follow.

"Is she family?" The nurse didn't make any attempt to mask his skepticism.

"She's my cousin." *Eighth, twice removed*? Something close to that.

The nurse studied them both, no doubt comparing Mandy's fair skin to Candace's olive for a moment before signaling Candace to follow.

Mandy endured the nurse's questions and having her vitals taken. She tried not to watch Candace's reaction to the story she related of how she injured her foot.

The nurse looked up from the computer he was using. "You climbed a fence wearing a skirt?"

"Hence the rip." Mandy toyed with the frayed edge of the ruined vintage '90s broomstick skirt.

The nurse raised his brow and continued typing.

As soon as he left, Candace pounced. "You didn't tell the nurse what startled you? DC? As in the famous, rich one whose grandfather owned the old mansion north of town?"

"Daniel Crawford came up behind me and accused me of trespassing."

"*The* Daniel Crawford? Is he as handsome as his photos?" Candace mock-fanned herself.

Didn't matter how handsome he was. Those piercing-blue eyes could not overcome his rudeness. Mandy didn't want to get into that now, so she shrugged.

Candace moved beside the gurney. "There has got to be more to the story than that."

Why isn't the doctor here yet? "Okay, how about he is the rudest, most bullheaded, most condescending, ungentlemanly person I have ever met. Grandma Mae would tan his hide if she could see him now."

Candace's penciled-in brows disappeared under her blue bangs.

Someone tapped on the door. A balding doctor stuck his head in. "Miss Fowler?"

"That's me." Anticipating his next question, Mandy rattled off her birth date like a prisoner in a French novel.

The doctor manipulated her foot one way, then another. "I don't think it's broken. Let's double-check with some X-rays."

An hour later she left the hospital with a large bandage on her elbow, a boot on her left foot, and a pair of crutches. Calcaneal fracture, fortunately a very small one, two to three weeks on crutches, and four to six in the boot. She headed toward her car, but Candace stopped her. "You can't drive."

"But I need to get my car home." Mandy leaned on the crutches. Thanks to a shot of some painkiller, the name of which escaped her, her heel no longer throbbed, but she did feel extraordinarily tired.

Candace guided Mandy to her green Saturn. "I'll come back with someone and get your car later. I can't believe you drove yourself here. And I can't believe he didn't offer to help you. You are right. He is a jerk."

Daniel scrolled through Mandy's public profile. There were photos with friends and roommates and a link to a blog featuring some of her portfolio. Digital arts were her forte, but she wasn't bad with a brush, either. Only a handful of selfies on another account. Most of the photos were of old buildings and architecture—evidence she'd told the truth about wanting to photograph the old place.

Shutting the browser, he got back to the reason he was here. What to do with the old mansion and nearly a square mile of land. Half of the land had been farmed in corn until the farmer he'd rented to had retired two years ago. The fifteen acres around the house had once been lovingly maintained. Now the roses and lilacs grew as wild as the forested areas his great-grandfather had set aside to be left in their natural state. The same great-grandfather stipulated the land could not be sold for one hundred years, the expiration date only weeks away, the anniversary date of some World War I battle he knew little about.

He flipped through the proposals. Although some were very lucrative, most of them would end up destroying the forested area. Only a couple of the proposals allowed him to subdivide the land. He hadn't considered them seriously until he recalled the summer spent playing in the pond, climbing trees, and counting clouds. Maybe if he tore down the house, he would enjoy the land. He heard some of the Amish farmers to the northeast were looking for farms for their sons. He could sell off the old farmland to them. But he wasn't sure how to even approach them with an offer. They wouldn't want the house either, but they might dismantle it.

The third paragraph on the second page of one proposal stood out. Why were the mineral rights specified in such detail?

three

MANDY SWUNG HER CRUTCHES DOWN the art department's narrow hallway, trying not to hit anything. The old building wasn't exactly disability friendly. She tapped on the last door.

"Open!"

Balancing on the crutches and holding her bags, she found turning the handle nearly impossible. Her hand slipped a second time, but the door opened anyway.

"Mandy? What happened?" Professor Christensen held the door for her.

Mandy slid the camera case from her shoulder. "I was taking pictures of the Crawford mansion, and something startled me."

"Did you get any decent shots?"

She shook her head. "Only one. I hope it will be good enough for me to finish the project."

"Only one?" The professor took a seat at his cluttered desk.

Mandy set the camera case on top of a stack of papers. "The camera fell when I did."

She bit her lip as her adviser unzipped the camera case. He pulled out the three pieces of the lens and the camera. "Do you have any idea how much this camera costs? How hard did you fall?"

Mandy sat in the only chair not piled with art books. "I looked the camera up last night. I guess I owe the university a big chunk of money." Mandy cringed. It would take almost three years of work to pay the debt off if she moonlighted and used all her savings. "I know I can't graduate if I owe the university any money."

He examined the camera parts, trying to fit them back together. "I'll talk to the dean and see what we can do about the camera. I assume there is some insurance policy, so you would only owe a portion, but even 10 percent would be a fair chunk of change."

She shifted in her seat, trying to find a more comfortable place for the boot.

Dr. Christensen put the camera parts back in the bag. "How are you at grant writing?"

"I wrote a couple as an undergrad, and I did one for the high school art department."

He sat back in his worn leather chair. "You might want to sharpen your pencil and see if you can get any grants, which will help. I'm not sure how the university works in these matters. How exactly did you come to fall?"

"I was sitting on the fence, and Daniel Crawford came up behind me and yelled. He accused me of working with some land developer. I guess the rumors are true about him selling the place." Mandy tried unsuccessfully to keep her voice light.

The professor brightened. "Daniel Crawford is in town? Any chance he'll help pay for the camera?"

She let out a harsh laugh. He wouldn't help her to the car—why would he hand over money?

"You could send C & O enterprises one of your grant proposals. They have donated to us before." He leaned forward, a hopeful gleam in his eye.

"I'm sure that would go over well. 'The *C* in C & O helped break this camera when I was almost trespassing on his land. Will you buy a new one for the university?'" Mandy read off an imaginary paper, balled it up, then sent it flying into the trash can.

The professor leaned back and laughed. "I don't know if that would work."

Mandy joined in the laughter.

"How is the project, then?" her mentor asked, coming around to the point of their meeting.

"The Crawford place is the last piece."

"Let's keep your schedule for your MFA show April 17 titled 'If Only...'? And hopefully we can work something out with the camera. At the very least you will still have all of your work done and only need to wait until the time the university can be paid to pick up your diploma." He gave Mandy a half smile. "It's one of the most original ideas I've seen the last several years. Be proud of yourself. Go home, work on your project, and I'll see you next week. Oh and have the descriptions completed for the printer by the first."

Mandy shook the professor's hand and left. For years she had wished on birthday candles to see Danny again. Too bad no one had told her ten-year-old self to be careful what she wished for. That didn't keep her from wishing for a miracle now. Between the single photo she had to work with and the money she owed, she would have been better off not even trying for her MFA. Her crutch caught on the exterior door as she left the building. At least she didn't fall.

four

DANIEL READ COLIN'S TEXT. **You win. She hasn't posted a thing. Bill is paid. Copay refunded.**

— **Thanks. Too bad we didn't bet. I want your car. You don't even drive the Lamborghini!**

The college graduation gift was a long-standing joke. Colin rarely drove, and when he did, he drove his "nondescript" vehicle.

Ha, ha. BTW, at the rate the social media is pinging in your area, it won't be long before the P'razzi descends. Stay away from the local diners, says Morgan!

— **Sorry, looking for someone.**

Not many out of towners visited the café and the diner. But neither did Mandy.

I can get her address …

— **Nope.** *Already got it.*

Daniel turned back to his computer. He wasn't sure why he didn't like the contract with the London-based ad agency. C & O's legal team assured him the wording was routine, but his gut told him otherwise. He'd ignored his sixth sense twice in the past year—first by not dumping Summerset sooner, and now with Amanda. But the leftover rage from finding a survey team on his property earlier that day had taken over. He should have followed his instincts when he'd felt she offered no threat, at least not to his property. His mind was a different story. She had been occupying far too much of his thoughts this week. But it was natural to want to check up on her welfare. Too bad she lived on a dead-end street, or he would drive by more often.

No way would he ignore his instincts in business, too. Hence the reason he'd spent his Saturday morning cross-referencing British law books. A half hour later his patience was rewarded. He highlighted a paragraph in the contract and emailed it back to legal. Most likely he would need to go to London next week. Once again, he'd created more work for himself.

Daniel opened the fridge. Dang. He'd finished the milk this morning. The freezer contained only two beat-up bags of frozen vegetables. A quick trip to the store was in order. Sitting in the cab of his truck at a four way, he realized he was still dressed for the video conference he'd held early that morning with several board members to debate the sale of the steel side of the company. He hoped he wouldn't stand out too much. There was one advantage of the small town—no resident paparazzi, and with so many Amish in the area, tourists would be staring at the stable in the parking lot, not looking for celebrities.

Mandy maneuvered across the parking lot on her crutches. Candace didn't need her input on the groceries, but she wanted to get out of the house. At least the big-box grocery store had motorized carts and she could choose her favorite ice cream. To her dismay, when they entered the store, all the motorized carts were in use.

Candace turned to Mandy. "Do you think you can make it? Do you want to go back and sit in the car?"

The checkout lines stood four customers deep. It would be too warm in the car for as long as Saturday shopping would take.

March had graced them with practically perfect spring weather. "I'll wait over there." She pointed her chin in the direction of the empty bench near the pharmacy.

"Sorry, I'll be back in a few." Candace disappeared down the card aisle.

"Don't forget the ice cream," she didn't yell as she knew Candace wouldn't hear over the crowd.

To pass the time, Mandy pulled out her phone and opened to her favorite social media site. The first picture in her feed was of Daniel Crawford eating at the local diner. Her friend had captioned the photo "Look who I saw today!!!!" Mandy scrolled down the page. A slew of DC sightings filled the screen. In most of the photos he appeared almost friendly, and, as always, his sandy hair was nothing short of model perfect.

She switched to her page and updated her status. "Crutches are not fun. Word of advice—careful what fences you choose to climb." She added a photo of her booted foot. It might help put off questions on Monday when she returned to work.

Her longtime roommate Tessa had posted more amazing photos of stained-glass cathedral windows in Vendôme, France. Repairing windows designed hundreds of years ago suited her history-buff roommate perfectly. It would've been a fun internship to snag. But Mandy had a contract to teach at the high school and knew very little about stained-glass beyond the introductory-level class she had taken.

"Miss Fowler."

She looked up to see one of her students approaching.

"What did you do for spring break?" The young man pulled off the hood to his navy sweatshirt like she insisted he do in class.

"I worked on my MFA project because, unlike you, I still had school."

"No, I mean what did you do for fun to hurt your foot—skydive?"

Mandy laughed at the teen's intense look. "No skydiving. Just working on my project."

"Wow, can you get hurt doing art?"

She gave him a smile. "You can if you are not very, very, careful."

"Zach! Zach!" called a woman pushing a cart with one toddler inside and another child hanging off the back.

Zach looked over his shoulder. "That's my mom. I better go. See ya Monday." He walked fast enough not to force his mother to call again but not fast enough to erase the frown on her face.

Mandy opened her favorite game app and moved the candy pieces from side to side. Out of her peripheral vision she noticed somebody with very nice shoes and dress pants standing beside her.

Danny. Every other man in the store wore jeans and tennis shoes, unless they were Amish. She raised her eyes from her phone.

He spoke as soon as she made eye contact. "I owe you an apology, I didn't realize you were hurt bad. I mean if I had, I would have helped you. I thought you were faking it."

"Why would I do that?" She fought the urge to say more.

Daniel sat down next to her. "I don't know. I was sure you were with one of the land developers. But that's before I realized who you were."

"You remember me now?"

"Yeah. Your parting comment about Grandma Mae ..." He shrugged and gave one of those half smiles always on the covers at the checkout stands. "Did you get the photo you needed for your class?"

She moved a few inches away. He unnerved her—and not the way the coach did at school. "It wasn't for a class. I needed the photo for my MFA project, and I only ended up with one photo, not as clear as I hoped."

"MFA in what?" He seemed genuinely interested.

"Master of fine arts in visual arts, digital emphasis. That photo is all that's standing between me and my degree." *Why is he being nice? Doesn't he see the people looking our way?* Too bad the boot and crutches kept her from joining Candace.

"Tell me about this project you're doing."

She fumbled with the phone before scrolling to a picture of the abandoned '50s gas station out on the old highway. "I'm creating an 'If Only...' theme using digital art to envision what the future could have been for various buildings if they'd had different owners or pasts. Like this old gas station on Highway 30. This is what it looks like today." She swiped to another photo of the same gas station, modernized, with cars and people going in and out. "Had the station not closed, it might look like this. Or what if someone had turned it into a race-car museum?" She flipped to the next photo. Vintage gas pumps gleamed, and a family walked toward the door from an adjacent parking lot where a field now lay fallow.

Daniel leaned over the little screen. "How many of these have you done?"

"Five different buildings. The mansion was supposed to be the sixth and final piece. I only got one shot—usually I have fifty or more to work with." She kept her voice even as she closed the photo app and scooted back. He hadn't intended to sabotage her project.

Daniel's face paled slightly. "Sorry. I should've handled the situation better. Your parting shot about Grandma Mae was perfect. But I was sure you were somebody else. Not a reason to treat anyone poorly. Even if you had been one of those leeches...If I let you in to take photos close range, would that help?"

She smiled. "To be honest, new photos might save the project. I'm in enough trouble as it is."

"What kind of trouble?" He leaned forward.

Mandy scooted another half-inch away. "The camera and telephoto lens will cost over $60,000 to replace. I can't graduate until it's paid off."

"Doesn't the school have insurance?" His eyebrows knit the same way they had when he was eight and she'd told him Grandma Mae didn't have cable.

"My faculty adviser is considering what insurance will cover. But he suggested I write grant proposals." For a moment, Mandy thought of hitting him up for a grant, but the request would be as laughable as it had been in Dr. Christensen's office.

He checked his watch. "What if you come out this afternoon, say, around three, and I'll let you in to take all the pictures you want."

Mandy bit her lip. "I'll have to bring my roommate. I can't drive until I'm off the painkillers."

Someone cleared their throat. "You ready to go?" Ice-blue curls framed the amused look on Candace's face. She must have been standing there for a while.

"Daniel this is Candace, my roommate. Candace, Daniel."

He stood and shook Candace's hand. Mandy wished Candace were standing closer to her so she could smack the starstruck expression off her face.

"Candace, Daniel invited me out to take better photos of his mansion. Can you give me a ride around three?"

Candace's gaze flicked from Daniel to Mandy and back. "I'm sorry. I have an appointment this afternoon."

Mandy tried not to glare. When they'd entered the store, their afternoon was completely free. On the drive over, they'd discussed going to their favorite thrift shop in hopes of finding another vintage broomstick skirt to replace the one destroyed on the gate.

"I'll pick you up if you trust me with your address," Daniel said.

Mandy opened her contacts page of her phone. "What's your number? I'll text it to you."

Daniel laughed. "That is about the most original line I've had anybody use to get ahold of my phone number."

She willed her blush to stay away. "I don't want your phone number for me. If I go missing, I want the police to know the last person I texted."

He studied her booted foot and crutches. "Understandable but unnecessary."

Candace burst into laughter as Daniel and Mandy exchanged information on their phones.

"I'll see you at three." He left in the direction of the deli.

Candace watched him go before turning her attention to Mandy. "I got ice cream in here. We better get home. I think there is enough melting going on."

Mandy ignored the comment, balanced herself on her crutches, and followed her roommate out of the store.

five

A MIDNIGHT-BLUE American-made pickup—not what Mandy expected. She let the blinds drop and turned to face Candace. "I thought you had an appointment."

"I do. Watching you go out with Daniel." Candace twirled the end of the hot-pink scarf tied around her head.

"You better make yourself scarce. He's coming up the walkway."

He'd changed into jeans and a T-shirt with the logo of an area restaurant. She went to open the door and stepped out to keep him from seeing Candace.

At the truck, Daniel held open the door. Mandy studied the high seat. If she didn't have the boot and crutches, it wouldn't be a problem.

"Let me help." He gathered the crutches and leaned them against the side of his truck. "It will be easier if you face me."

Mandy was still puzzling over his words when he placed his hands on her waist and lifted her into the cab. He stepped back, but the warmth remained where his hands had been. She managed to mutter a thank-you as he handed her the crutches before closing the door.

Without another word, he got in and started the truck. Still feeling his hands about her, Mandy struggled to come up with a topic of conversation. *Do all women feel like this when you pay attention to them?* Hardly seemed like an appropriate topic. Her "Nice day" was met by a "yup," reminding her more of the stoic little boy of twenty years ago. He'd started talking after she'd taught him to catch frogs.

Daniel navigated out of her neighborhood and to the county road leading toward the mansion. If one of them didn't start talking soon, the drive would be unbearable. Mandy searched for a topic of conversation. It had been nearly twenty years since they'd spent the summer searching for tadpoles in his creek and eating popsicles stolen from his freezer. Back then he'd been the boy on the other side of the fence. Now he was one of the most sought-after men in the country, and she was still the kid from the tiny house.

Daniel didn't seem inclined to speak either. At least he wasn't holding a gun on her.

At the gate he hopped out, unlocked it, and drove through. Then he went and locked the gate again. "Where do you need to go to get your photo?"

"Anyplace where the old walnut tree isn't in the way. I need the architecture from the east wing. The gingerbread work is hard to duplicate in my mind."

The road curved around the tree.

"Right here would be perfect."

Daniel stopped the truck. She started to open her door, but he laid his hand on her arm. "Wait for me to come around. I'd hate for you to put those crutches in some gopher hole."

She studied him. Without the anger, he reminded her of the shy eight-year-old who'd escorted her on a tour of the mansion. She tried not to read anything into the hands on her waist and removed her hand from his shoulder as soon as her toes touched the ground.

He carried her bag while she found the right spot. Mandy exchanged her crutches for the bag.

"That camera isn't as nice as the one you had the other day."

She raised the camera. "This is my camera. The broken one belongs to the university. I borrowed the camera for the telephoto lens—now I'm out $60,000."

"You mean six, don't you? I thought I heard wrong at the store."

Mandy took a shot. "Nope, sixty. Six-zero, zero, zero, zero. Which, for a third-year high school teacher, is twice my salary. If the university insurance doesn't come through, I may never get the diploma. Ironically, with the degree, my pay would go up $10k." She snapped two more photos.

He gave a low whistle.

She took a few hops, mindful of not putting her weight on the booted foot, then a couple more, raised her camera, and took a few shots before taking a few more jumps and repeating the process. Daniel offered a steadying hand on her elbow whenever she stopped. They had moved nearly the length of a football field before she put the camera back in her bag. "I have what I need now. Thank you."

"Do you need to go inside?" Daniel exchanged the bag for her crutches.

She shook her head. "No, I'm only fixing up the outside of the buildings. Besides, I like the memories I have of that summer. I'm sure the inside has deteriorated as much as the outside, and I don't want to remember that."

Daniel stiffened. "That was the worst summer of my life. I'd like to forget what the inside of the house looks like." He grabbed her bag and headed back to the truck, leaving her to navigate the gopher holes and ant hills herself.

She watched his retreating form. What had happened to her Danny? She was sure she had seen the polite boy only minutes ago. They had had so much fun that summer. How could it be the worst ever?

Being around Mandy brought back too many memories too fast. He shouldn't have left her there, but crying in front of her wasn't an option and he feared he might. He opened the cab door and looked back. Mandy had barely covered ten feet. Driving on the weedy lawn wouldn't hurt, so he started the truck and drove to her side.

He might not be the most perceptive of men, but when he lifted Mandy onto the truck seat, he was fairly sure she was confused and in pain. He shouldn't have walked off without a word. But the thoughts of his mother had been overwhelming.

"Sorry about that. I try not to think about that summer. Seeing you brought back a lot of memories, many of them bad. I shouldn't have said it was the worst summer because it was also the best. I did meet the first friend I ever had." He offered what he hoped was an apologetic smile before shutting her door.

Mandy waited to speak until he put his seat belt on. "*A Tale of Two Cities* summer, then? It was the best of times; it was the worst of times."

"That fits." Not only had he lost his mom, but his father had died in some measure with her.

"It was kind of like that for me too. I realized my parents didn't want me around. Little kids and archeology don't go together well. Don't get me wrong—they loved me. They just didn't want me with them."

"I thought your parents had taken you on digs before."

They passed two farmhouses before she responded. "They did, but the year before, I was playing at a dig and a scorpion stung me. Fortunately, one of their students decided to investigate my screaming. My mom had heard me but figured I was playing. Hence my summers with Grandma Mae. Not that I understood my being at the dig was a safety issue. I thought they didn't want me around."

He nodded, having adults not wanting him around was all-too familiar and probably the reason he'd bonded with the scruffy little tomboy and her grandmother. "Do they still teach?"

"They are in Peru on a joint sabbatical. I think they spend more time below the equator than above it. They love their work, and I think they wish I were more interested. But, alas, I hate scorpions and learned to prefer skirts over pants. Neither of which work well on digs." Mandy laughed, a tiny sound not quite sincere.

Daniel nodded. "Did you ever go on another dig?"

"No, when I was sixteen, they asked me to, but I wasn't interested. Especially after all Dad's caveats about staying away from the college boys. It was like he was sure I would lead them to their doom or they would lead me to mine."

At a stop sign, Daniel looked her way. "I see why your father might have been concerned."

She blushed. His heart did a little flip. When was the last time he'd seen a woman blush? Not one of the fake actress ones, but a real, honest-to-goodness, blood-rushing-to-the-cheeks sort of blush?

"What about you? Is your life as glamorous as it seems?"

"Ten minutes of my life each week manages to find its way into the gossip columns. What they miss is the hours I spend in boardrooms, sorting out ideas and trying to listen to people twice my age who may or may not be trying to give me good advice about the empire the last four generations of Crawfords built. Then everyone I meet thinks they know me because they have seen my photo while standing in the checkout line. I get invited to big parties where people usually try to part me with large amounts of my money. Other than some delicious food, I would say my life isn't as idyllic as it seems."

He drove by the ice cream shop. "Do you want to stop and get a cone?"

"Can I take a rain check? I really would like to put my foot up. I chose not to take my last pill before we left, and I'm regretting it."

Daniel winced. "And then I left you to navigate back to the truck on your own. Grandma Mae would stand me in a corner for a month."

"But she would give you cookies afterward. If you want ice cream, Candace picked some up today. You can come in and have a bowl."

Daniel parked in the driveway. "I'd love to."

Candace dashed out of the living room as they entered the house.

"Wasn't her hair a different color this morning? And shorter?" Daniel tried to make sense of the flowing auburn locks he'd seen.

"Yup, I think she has sixteen or more different wigs. You will be hard-pressed to catch her in the same hair two days in a row."

Not sure where to go with the conversation, he turned to Mandy's needs. "Why don't you get comfortable, and I'll bring you your pain meds. Where do you keep them?"

She sat on the couch. "In the cupboard above the refrigerator—the green bin. There should be one left in the Rx bottle."

Daniel had never seen a kitchen like this. The cabinets were painted in a dozen mini canvases, each one its own work of art. He found the drinking glasses in a Monet-inspired cupboard next to a Matisse. Above the sink hung a stained-glass window reminiscent of a Tiffany lamp. The cup in his hand overflowed while he was taking it all in.

"That kitchen is amazing! Who did you get to do that?"

Mandy swallowed the pill before responding. "That's what happens when you have a house full of artists and no dates on the weekends. It's a work in progress. Over the years, six or seven of us have added our work to the room. I'm not sure how the painting got started. The Albrecht Dürer was here when I moved in, as was the kitchen table."

"I missed the table. Your landlord doesn't mind?"

"No, it's Candace's house, and she is pretty much the instigator. As long as we follow her rules, she is pretty cool with everything."

"She has rules?" Daniel took the empty glass.

"Yes, yes, I do."

He turned toward the voice. This time her hair was in a blonde bob.

Candace struck a pose worthy of a Grecian goddess. "Go ahead and ask. I know you are dying to."

"What's up with the wigs?"

"Every year I get a cancer free checkup, I buy a new wig. I already have my eye on the one I am going to get in June, my tenth. My father and sister also give them to me for birthdays and Christmas. I have seventeen. Plus a few cheap ones for fun."

"If you've been cancer free for almost ten years, why do you still wear wigs?"

"Alopecia. After my chemo ended, my hair didn't grow back. At first my mother got me natural wigs. But I decided to have some fun. Hence, tonight I'm a blonde off to a party at a friend's. So, what are you two kids doing?" Candace gathered her purse.

Mandy answered. "I invited Daniel in for some ice cream."

"What? No takeout and a movie?" Candace's idea sounded great to Daniel.

"Just don't forget the rules. Bye, kids." She flitted out the door.

"What rules?"

"This is a smoke and alcohol-free house. If you want to know why—the cancer is part of it, and the details are for Candace to tell. It's also drug free. Usually we don't even have anything stronger than ibuprofen, but Candace insisted." Mandy pointed to the empty Rx bottle.

"Okay, I guess I will not decide to start smoking while I am here. Chinese or pizza?"

Mandy shifted her position on the couch to raise her foot. "Do you mind burgers? When I'm in pain, I always want cheeseburgers and chocolate milkshakes."

"Your wish is my command. Would you like fries with that?"

"Sure, and let yourself in when you come back, okay?"

"Are you sure it's safe to leave the door unlocked?"

"This isn't Chicago. I'm sure I'll be safe for the twelve and a half minutes it will take you to go get burgers."

Pain was evident in the tightness around her eyes, and Daniel was sure she was trying to use humor to help ease it. "Okay, start the timer."

six

LIGHT SNORING FILLED THE LIVING room as Daniel walked into the house. He set the takeout bags in the kitchen. He'd been absent more than double the twelve-minute limit. It would have been much faster to go in and order, as everyone else in town wanted to get burgers too. For a moment, he debated letting Mandy sleep, but shakes set in the freezer never tasted quite the same as fresh. He'd get her to eat and then leave so she could rest. He made as much noise as possible setting out their food, but the snoring continued.

He studied her sleeping form. Her ponytail hung off the side of the couch, her hair had darkened over the years. Against the tan leather, the color reminded him of the line of cinnamon sugar he helped dribble on the rolls Grandma Mae used to make. The thought of waking her Sleeping-Beauty style crossed his mind. But he was nowhere near the true-love's-kiss stage of the relationship. If he didn't have the whole lawsuit mess, could he be? He'd like the chance to try.

He settled on touching her shoulder. "The food is here."

Her eyes opened slowly—brown, soft, and dreamy. A tiny smile curved her lips, almost as if she had been awoken by a kiss.

Mandy blinked a few times. "Oh. I guess I was more tired than I thought." She took Daniel's offered hand and sat up, scooting back to keep her injured foot on the couch.

He motioned to her foot. "Shall I bring the food in here?"

"If you wouldn't mind. I'd rather not put my boot back on."

"What exactly did you do to it?" Daniel headed for the kitchen.

"Well, I was trying to take a photo when—" Mandy stopped when he turned back.

He raised his brows and gave her his half smile. "I meant is it broken, sprained, or torn?"

She smiled. "The doctor says I broke my foot—a calcaneus fracture on the bottom of my heel. It's also known as a 'Lover's Fracture' because men get them jumping from windows or balconies avoiding their lovers' spouses. But don't spread that around. I wouldn't want anyone to get the wrong idea. I was lucky—mine is fairly small. Four weeks and I should be out of this in time for my MFA exhibit."

He arranged the food on plates in the kitchen and smiled at the name Lover's Fracture, but he didn't want her running from him. He carried two plates to the coffee table. "How bad does it hurt?"

"Not as bad as it did on Tuesday. I hope by Monday I'll only need a couple ibuprofen to make it through the day."

"What happens on Monday?"

"Spring break is over. So I get to try not to lose my patience with my art students as they readjust to life."

Daniel hurried to grab their shakes. "You're teaching and going to the university?"

"I don't have any classes now other than my final project, which isn't a class, per se. It's more of a 'meet with my adviser every Thursday to critique what I did the past week.'"

"When will you graduate?" He took a chair at the end of the couch nearest Amanda.

"My show is mid-April. I should graduate May 22nd. But the university will hold my diploma until I pay off the camera." Mandy gave a half smile and took a bite of her burger.

Daniel was half surprised she hadn't asked him to pay for the broken camera, but then, Grandma Mae wouldn't have either. Women usually wanted his money. How long would it be before she asked? He didn't think she would. He should offer. He changed the subject. "Are you still up for a movie, or would you rather finish your nap?"

Mandy dipped a fry in her shake. "With this much sugar, I won't be able to sleep. There is a DVD collection in the drawer under the TV, or we have streaming."

He rifled through the collection and pulled out an old Disney movie. "I haven't seen this since we were kids."

"It is the same one. I have all of Grandma Mae's old movies, including the VHS tapes. Remember how I had to know what apple dumplings tasted like?"

"I think we talked my cook and Grandma Mae into both making a batch on the same day. I thought I would never need to eat again." He held up the DVD. "Do you want to see it?"

Her mouth full of fries, Mandy nodded.

The last few bars of the theme song played as Mandy woke to Daniel's gentle nudging.

"Hey, sleepyhead." At least his face wasn't as close this time. He'd replaced the pillow propping up her foot halfway through the movie when she told him she needed to ice it.

Trying to stretch without looking like she was stretching, she sat up straighter.

"Will you hand me my boot and crutches?" She slid the boot on. Daniel stood and cleared the remains of their dinner while Mandy slipped down the hall to the bathroom.

When she returned, the living room was straightened. Even the DVD was put away. She sighed. He had cleaned up and disappeared. She heard water in the kitchen sink running and followed the sound. "Thanks. You didn't need to do the dishes."

"And miss an excuse to spend more time in this kitchen? At first I thought none of the plates matched because you got the free ones at the end of garage-sale days, but it is deliberate, isn't it?"

Mandy leaned into her crutches. "A little of both."

"Is the rest of the house this way? Other than the living room, it is so—"

"Boringly normal after the kitchen?"

Daniel dried his hands on a towel and turned to face her. "Not exactly the way I would have put it."

"Do you want a tour?"

"Are you up to giving one?" He pointed to her crutches.

"Sure, but I'll warn you, the house is a maze. The main part dates back to the sixties, but sometime in the eighties it got added on twice. Then, when Candace got ahold of it, she moved a wall or two. The hallway circles around the entire place."

Mandy continued through the kitchen to the eating area.

"Who are Tessa and Araceli?" Daniel traced the names painted on the placemats.

"Our roommates. Tessa is in Europe on a stained-glass apprenticeship, and Araceli is recovering from a nasty case of mono at home in Massachusetts. Since they plan on coming back, they still have rooms here. It is quiet this semester."

They entered a hallway. To one side a glass door opened into a sunroom filled with easels, and canvases. Cupboards lined one wall. "This is our studio. Candace's father designed the room with controllable blinds and special lighting, so we can paint day or night. There is also a separate air-filter system, so she can oil paint or even airbrush without fumes entering the main house."

They passed two closed doors, their chalkboard nameplates declaring the rooms to be occupied by the missing roommates.

"This is the Nemo bathroom." Mandy pushed open a door labeled "Mermaids only."

Daniel stepped into the room. "It looks like every animated movie with an ocean scene is in here. Hey, is that Mr. Limpet?"

"Wow, no one ever notices him, but then most people didn't watch movies with Grandma Mae. The Nautilus is in the corner behind the toilet, but no squid. You'll notice the jetted tub is in Ariel's cave."

Daniel came out of the bathroom and preceded Mandy down the hall. He stopped inches from walking into a wall.

She laughed. "*Trompe-l'œil* means 'deceive the eye.' That is my hallway to nowhere."

Daniel touched the wall as if trying to prove his eyes were wrong, then turned to face Mandy. "You let me go first deliberately, didn't you? Wait a second—your hallway to nowhere?"

"First thing I painted when I moved in." Mandy turned the corner he'd missed.

The hallway opened into a bookshelf-lined room with two wing-back chairs. Little tables with lamps completed the library. A wrought-iron stairway circled up in the center. Mandy used her crutch to point to it. "Take a peek."

After a couple of minutes, he came back down. "Those bean-bags are fabulous."

"We have a view of the stars most nights, too. I love to read up there." Mandy hoped he hadn't caught her blush. Kimberly, the roommate Mandy had replaced, had dubbed the space "Lover's Loft." The roommates were usually discreet when using it and warned each other off by placing a particular book on the table at the entrance of the library. Mandy had yet to use her chosen book.

Turning another corner, they passed Candace's door.

"This is the other bathroom." Painted to mimic a roman bath complete with marble statues and a Mediterranean view, the room represented more dateless weekends than Mandy would ever admit.

Daniel gave a low whistle. "This must have taken awhile. The painting makes the room seem huge."

"We started painting our sophomore year. I didn't live here yet, but I would crash whenever Uncle George visited Grandma Mae. He made it a point to come every other weekend to fulfill his duty. Drove me crazy, always bossing me around like a two-year-old. Painting this was my therapy."

Pausing at her bedroom door, Daniel asked, "May I?"

"You'll be disappointed."

He walked in and turned around twice. "This looks almost like your attic room at Grandma Mae's. Even the pictures on the walls."

"Uncle George let me keep whatever I wanted from the house other than the silverware and silver tea set his now-ex-wife wanted. The rest of the things I liked are in storage. Mandy turned down the next hall. "Come on, the only thing left is the basement and for you to sign the laundry room."

She stood at the top of the stairs, the thought of going up and down them with the crutches paralyzing her. "Turn right when you go down."

"Aren't you coming?"

"If I go down, I must come back up, and I'm not good with my crutches."

Daniel turned his back to her. "Piggyback?"

She hesitated.

"Come on. I won't drop you."

Halfway down the stairs, Mandy knew she'd made a big mistake. The tingling of her nerves had nothing to do with the fear of being dropped. Her dreams and fears were colliding. She'd never denied she was attracted to Daniel Crawford, but so were half the women with Internet access.

Vintage movie posters decorated the large multipurpose room, which housed a ping-pong table, treadmill, and exercise bike. Instead of setting her down, he walked around the perimeter, stopping to study the posters. He paused and turned slowly around. "This room doesn't have any windows."

"The basement doesn't have any. Candace thought about putting some in, but it was too expensive in the end."

The next door was labeled "Tornado shelter."

"Really?"

"It isn't decorated. You know, most of the houses around here have basements. Candace made hers more official. She grew up farther south, where tornadoes are an annual occurrence." Mandy wasn't fond of the little room. Fortunately she'd only had to use it twice. "On to the laundry room."

They entered the brightly painted blue-and-white room. Cupboards and counters lined one wall, and the other wall had a large washer and dryer, wash sink, and clothes hanger. The back wall was painted black and decorated with graffiti.

"The back wall is a chalkboard. Everyone who completes a tour must add something to the wall and sign it. There are chalk pens in the basket."

Daniel set Mandy down on top of the counter and turned to face her, trapping her. Her heart sped up. If this were any other guy, she would be in full defensive mode. She pointed to the basket. "There are colored chalks too."

He stepped back slowly, stretching some invisible band contacting them until it released her. He rummaged through the basket and selected a white and a blue marker.

She couldn't see around him to see what he had drawn. "What did you write?"

He shook his head. "You'll have to wait until you can walk to find out." Ignoring her protests, he picked her up and carried her back upstairs.

It shouldn't feel this good to be in his arms. It was exhilarating and relaxing all at once. Mandy tried to stifle a yawn—as well as her attraction to him.

"That is my cue to go. Thanks for the fun evening." He set her down at the top of the stairs, holding her until she had her balance. Then he stepped away and handed her the crutches.

"Good night, Amanda." He gave her arm a little squeeze and left.

She watched the reflection of the headlights as he maneuvered the truck out of the driveway. And another point for the friend zone. Nothing wrong with that. They had been friends. Why should that change now? The pain meds must be playing with her mind, filling it with impossibilities.

seven

NEVER HAD MANDY BEEN SO relieved to reach her prep hour. The first day after spring break was enough to make every high school teacher wish the holiday had never happened. One student swiped a crutch and used it to mimic a machine gun, prompting Mandy to lock them in the supply closet. She scooted herself around the room on her rolling chair. Her third-hour class was more rambunctious than usual, if that were possible. She confiscated two of Roderigo's cartoons depicting other students in terms the school board would call bullying. Writing up the incident took her most of the students' drawing time. Too bad the kid had talent. If he'd use it productively, he could go far. She watched the clock as if it were the last day of school. Finally, the bell rang, and the students filed out of the room to inflict their exuberance on another teacher.

Somehow Mandy kept her cheering silent. Caught up on her grading, she pulled up the pictures she'd taken on Saturday at the Crawford place with Daniel.

The fourth was perfect. Immediately she opened the photo manipulation program and started to correct the image. Magnified, the roof displayed more damage than she noticed through the viewfinder. Probably from the same tornado that had destroyed

Grandma Mae's house three and a half years ago. Why hadn't Daniel repaired it? It wasn't as if he lacked the funds for a new roof and insurance would pick up most of the tab. Were all those trunks still stored in the attic? The treasures carefully packed away almost a century ago were no doubt moldering. They had only ever opened a few of the trunks, but the yellow Jackie O-style ball gown still called to her. Anger flashed. How could Danny be so irresponsible?

The digital repairs to her photo brought the house in line with the well-maintained building of her memories. Summers spent with Grandma Mae shone as the brightest spots in her young life. Each year, she spent two glorious months alone with Grandma Mae while her parents traveled to some foreign location on a dig. At the time, she hadn't understood the need to go make holes in the ground. Grandma Mae's garden provided more than enough opportunity to dig to her heart's delight, gorge herself on peas straight from the pod, and peer over the fence at the huge house next door with its sixty rooms to Grandma Mae's six.

Despite Grandma's warnings, Mandy had slipped through the fence in search of the lone boy who dressed far too nice to be throwing rocks in the pond. She hadn't found him, but Grandma Mae had found her and marched her down the long drive to the house, the following day.

Grandma Mae knocked on the massive door. A uniformed maid ushered them into an office where an old man sat hunched over a desk, surrounded by piles of paper.

He stared down her grandma. "Miss Mae, what is this about my grandson needing to have a friend?"

"Now, Dan, you can't keep the boy locked up with whatever computer game you gave him all summer. It isn't healthy for him. You have some of the best climbing trees on this side of the state. Let him go out and play."

The old man stared at Grandma Mae for what seemed like an eternity but didn't move.

Grandma took a firm grip on Mandy's shoulder and pushed her forward. "This is my Mandy. She will do him a world of good. Even teach him to fish. What do you say?"

"He doesn't want to fish. Doesn't want to do anything."

"What he needs is a friend. I recall my Peter telling me tales of you needing one once."

"That was a very long time ago."

"I think you will find the needs of little boys haven't changed much in seven decades."

The old man grunted. "If it stops him from crying every night, they can play together, but if he gets worse, she goes."

Mandy had prayed every night that Danny wouldn't cry.

Sitting back and pulling herself out of her reminiscing, she surveyed her work. A start, but then this was the easy one.

The noise level increased outside of her door. She checked the clock —lunch, with a chaser of ibuprofen.

After retrieving her crutches from the supply closet, she went to the teachers' lounge and popped her leftover lasagna into the microwave.

"How did you earn crutches?" The school's football coach leaned on the counter, studying more than her foot. She had spent most of the semester dodging his advances. Didn't spring training start soon? Or was that baseball?

"Just a lucky break." The microwave bell dinged, and Mandy slid her food out. The room was uncommonly empty. Now she had a real dilemma—hot lasagna and crutches. "Would you mind putting this on a table?"

Coach Robb lumbered over to the table near the window. She should have been more specific as to which table. He put her food down and held out a chair for her, then took the seat next to her.

"I think the trainer has one of those scooters in the athletic room." He reached over and touched her hand. "I am sure I can arrange for you to borrow it."

Mandy slid her hand out from under his and picked up her fork. "Thanks, Coach." She emphasized his title. "Do you think I could keep the kids from running off with it?"

This time he touched her shoulder. "How many times have I asked you to call me Dirk?"

Dirk the jerk. Hoping to dislodge his hand, Mandy shrugged her shoulder.

Dirk shook his head. "I doubt the kids will leave it alone. I have enough problems with the football players who need it."

"I seem to be getting along well enough with my crutches, but if I decide I need your scooter, I'll be sure and ask." Mandy shoveled a too-large bite into her mouth.

"Careful there, darling. You don't want to choke." This time his hand found her knee.

She brushed it off and tried to scoot back but was penned in by the window and the wall. Where were the other teachers? "I need to finish something before my next class. Will you dump this for me?" At least she had an apple in her room. His fingers returned to rubbing lightly above her knee. Mandy picked his hand up and moved it back to the top of the table as one of the math teachers walked in.

The teacher raised her brows and turned to the fridge. Mandy fumbled with her crutches and stood, looking for a speedy exit, but Dirk caught her by the wrist, causing her crutch to wobble. "No reason to rush off. You barely got three bites in."

"I really need to go. Thanks for the offer of the scooter." Mandy hobbled out of the lounge as fast as she could. She would have felt bad about leaving Mrs. Bradly alone with Coach Robb, but Mr. Bradly was the wrestling coach, so she would be safe enough.

eight

DANIEL HIT THE INTERCOM BUTTON. "Bonnie, can you find the numbers of the photographers who tried to help Ms. Vandemark?"

"Yes, Mr. Crawford, and I have the confirmation for your trip to London. The service will be here at 4:00 p.m. tomorrow to take you to O'Hare. I hope you don't mind—business class was full, I put you in first." Daniel didn't, he wasn't nearly as uptight about spending a few extra dollars as his grandfather had been. Bonnie had worked for both his father and grandfather and tried to maintain their miserly standards. When Daniel visited the office as a child, she would sneak him candy. She often talked about retiring, but he kept giving her raises and more vacation time.

"I'm happy you found a flight to accommodate the meetings, and I won't complain about wasting money when it was my fault and I get extra room on a red-eye."

"I think the photographers are named in the police report."

"Thanks, Bonnie."

Daniel turned back to his computer. The compromise contracts his legal team had drafted looked solid. Thankfully they had limited themselves to one apologetic email about missing the clause regarding using his image for the British firm's advertising purposes. The ad agency had tried to backpedal. Hence the reason he was meeting with them on Wednesday afternoon and their competitor on Thursday morning. With any luck, he could fly back on Friday and be at the Indiana property for the weekend before he had to deal with the courts in New York. He wanted to see Mandy again. Even if now was not a convenient time to start a relationship.

What was he thinking?

Renewing a friendship—that was all he was doing. No matter how fun or attractive he found Amanda, friendship was the extent of it. He'd plotted out the possibilities of a relationship on a spreadsheet after arriving back in Chicago early yesterday morning. Logically each one failed, but logic was not doing a good job at overruling his heart. But his current plan had nothing to do with his heart. It had everything to do with being a decent human.

Bonnie tapped on the door before entering. "One of the photographers is Vic Jamison. His primary residence is listed as Park Ridge. Did you know he was local?"

"I think he mentioned it." Daniel reached for the paper she held. Instead of handing it to him, she turned, closed the door, and took her favorite chair to the side of his desk.

"I'm not leaving until you tell me what's going on. And don't tell me it's about the old place and land developers. Usually when you take a few days down at the property you come back focused and refreshed. This time you are all wound up."

Daniel had two choices. He could tell her the truth now or wait until she wrung the details out of him. "I met an old friend, and the reunion didn't go very well."

"Does this have anything to do with the medical-bill payment Colin sent through to the private account?"

Of course she saw it. Why hadn't he called her last week?

"It's the little girl from that summer, isn't it? I thought I recognized the name." Bonnie stared at him for a moment. "Only she doesn't match your memories of the mud-pie making tomboy, does she? Glory be! I see retirement coming faster than I thought." Bonnie practically jumped from her seat.

"You have it all wrong. There is no way a relationship would fly. I tried to work it out on four different spreadsheets."

"Love is not a business merger. You can't plot out a risk-benefit analysis, because there are factors that defy even the most complicated mathematical formulas."

"I am not in love." Then why had he written that quote in the laundry room? 'Good fences make good neighbors but lousy lovers.' He started out writing the first half, a Robert Frost line familiar to the area due to its use at the Menno-Hof Mennonite Amish Visitor Center in Shipshewana, but then he'd pictured the new, unclimbable fence that replaced the old pole one at the estate and added the last part.

"But you are afraid you may be if given time, right?"

Daniel leaned back and contemplated the ceiling. If he had laser vision, he'd make the fire sprinkler go off to cool this conversation down. "Twenty years has built a huge fence in our lives. I don't know where to go." He let out a sigh. "May I have the photographer's information? And no, it has nothing to do with the Vandemark mess. It is about a broken camera."

Bonnie laid the paper on the desk. "One year, Daniel, and I am out of here and off to the little place in Arizona whether or not you have found another way to guard your door against all the single females in the building."

"Thanks, Bonnie, you are a gem."

"Don't you forget it. One year, Daniel. One year."

Marriage. Bonnie was convinced a change in his marital status would stop the stream of women trying to wheedle their way into his life.

Daniel pulled into a parking spot in front of the camera store Vic had suggested. Now he just needed to stay in the store long enough for the photographer to set up and get the exclusive shot he wanted, a fair trade.

Fortunately for Daniel, the "leaked photo" would serve a dual purpose. First, by confusing those whose livelihoods depended on keeping people like him in the headlines, and second, by informing the one person he needed to know that not everything was what it seemed. If he didn't see her this weekend, she needed to understand before he went to New York.

"Mr. Crawford, welcome to my little shop. Vic called me and gave me an idea of what you were looking for, and I pulled out a few models for you to inspect." The owner's smile indicated he knew he had a sure sale.

Forty-five minutes later, Daniel's phone vibrated with Vic's text.

Sorry—traffic. Ready when you are.

— Thanks

Daniel ended his impromptu photography lesson and walked to his car to the click, click, click of Vic's camera.

nine

By the time her Tuesday prep period came, Mandy's students had mostly returned to their less-active selves. Today she'd brought a sandwich for lunch so she could eat at her desk. When the lunch bell rang, she continued working on the windows of the mansion.

Near the end of the hour, her phone rang. She struggled to understand the excited voice on the other end.

"A new lens and camera were donated?" Mandy resisted the urge to recheck the phone to make sure the call was really from Professor Christensen.

"It showed up this morning in the dean's office by special carrier. No return address. Campus security swarmed the place, thinking the package might be a bomb since it wasn't delivered to central receiving." Dr. Christensen chuckled. "They were ready to send it through the X-ray and a bunch of other tests until I pointed out it was an original Nikon box with the seals still intact. They still cleared the office while the one officer volunteered to open it."

"Any idea who sent it?" Mandy tossed the remains of her lunch in the trash.

"No. Since it wasn't a bomb, security stopped trying to find the guy who'd made the delivery. Did you get any of the grant requests out?"

"I only finished writing them this morning. I was going to email them for your approval." Mandy closed the mansion photo.

"It is odd that someone would donate to the university in a way that wouldn't get them a tax deduction. Eighty thousand isn't exactly a small gift."

"Eighty? I thought the replacement cost sixty." Mandy jotted the number on a pad. So many circles.

"Newer camera and better lens."

"Wow." Mandy sat back in her chair.

"Since we have no idea where it came from, the dean decided you don't owe the school any money. I think he is happy not to have to aggressively pursue the insurance claims."

The bell rang.

"Thanks for calling, Dr. Christensen. My next class is going to begin. I'll see you Thursday." Mandy disconnected the call as the first few students bounded into the art room.

Candace removed the black plastic microwave tray from Mandy's hands and replaced it with her tablet. "Check this out."

Daniel's face filled the screen. Mandy set the tablet on the couch next to her. "I'm not interested in seeing any more of Daniel Crawford." Maybe if she ignored him, the microscopic crush would shrivel up and die.

"Read the headline." Candace sat down next to Mandy and picked the tablet up.

"If You Can't Beat 'em, Join 'em: DC Buys Paparazzi-Worthy Camera." Mandy took the tablet from her roommate's hand.

Daniel Crawford was spotted exiting a high-end

Chicago-area camera store Monday evening. According to our sources, he purchased a camera and telephoto lens valued at more than $80k after spending approximately an hour talking with the store owner, who declined to comment.

DC has been rather vocal about his distaste for the paparazzi since the Summerset Vandemark incident last December, calling for stronger ethics and privacy guidelines for the industry, including those who buy and publish photos.

Several of the photographers who took pictures of an apparently inebriated Summerset Vandemark after her fall at a New York City hotel before New Year's are facing charges for assault after blocking emergency medical personnel at the scene. The trial is set for early April, as well as a suit against the hotel by Miss Vandemark. Mr. Crawford is expected to be a key witness in both trials. Close sources claim she was at the hotel with Mr. Crawford, who was not present at the time of her accident but arrived in time to render assistance.

Rumors persist that the couple has not separated. Despite the fact, Daniel has been seen publicly with several women since mid-January, including Summerset at an Academy Awards after-party where witnesses report she dumped Daniel in a drunken rage.

Is Daniel trying to maintain his relationship with the socialite, disguised as one of the photographers who follows her every move, or is he doing research for the upcoming trial? We hope to have all the answers for you as the trial begins next week.

Mandy handed the tablet back.

"Well?" asked Candace.

"Well, what? He bought a camera. He is a billionaire; he buys lots of things." Mandy tried to shrug off the question.

"The night before, a camera of the same value is mysteriously donated to the Art and Design school?"

She refused to be baited. "Coincidence."

Candace huffed. "Seriously? Are you blind? He bought the camera for you."

Mandy shook her head. "I told you, when he left Saturday evening, friend zone, remember?"

"Uh-huh. You keep telling yourself that." Candace got up. "New topic—first date with the law student I met last week. Scarf or wig?"

Mandy pondered the options. "What did you have on when you met him?"

Candace tugged on the ends of the scarf she wore. "I think I wore the short brunette—no, the blonde."

"Go with the redhead. It will be a big enough change but not shocking. It should get you into the conversation if you want to go there." Mandy picked her meal back up. "I guess I am on my own tonight. Bless the woman who invented frozen dinners."

Candace turned on the news while she dressed for her date. Mandy finished the last couple bites of chicken, chucked the empty microwave-meal container into the trash, and moved to her combination studio-bedroom to work on her project. Her giant Wacom screen was her version of Nirvana. Before the first song finished playing on her feed, Mandy was in the zone, replacing overgrown weeds with green lawn—and reminiscing. Flying kites, running on the perfect lawn in bare feet.

Candace popped her head in the door. "Guess who is on TV next?"

"I don't want to hear it." Mandy covered her ears in jest.

The doorbell rang.

"That's my date. Don't wait up."

Mandy sat back and studied her work. The notes of a popular entertainment show drifted in from the other room. Candace had left the TV on again.

It took Mandy a minute to track down the remote. The bleach-blonde announcer started into her first story. "Is Daniel Crawford joining the paparazzi?" The same photo of Daniel carrying a bag with the photography-store logo used in the story she read earlier flashed across the screen. The blonde turned to her cohost. "What do you think DC will do with an $80,000 camera?"

Mandy shut the TV off. Candace was probably right. The camera at the school was purchased by Daniel last night. Her phone chimed Candace's tone, then stopped. Mandy checked the screen. Pocket dial. She double-checked her text messages just to be sure. Daniel's name appeared at the bottom of the screen from the Saturday text exchange. She opened a text window.

Hey, did you give—
Delete, delete, delete.
There was a camera donated to the uni—
Delete, delete, delete.
Thank you for donating the camera. I can graduate now. Thanks.
Send.

She waited a moment, then pocketed her phone. It beeped.
— How did you figure it out?
Tabloids are often wrong. Mandy left off the question mark.
— Good call.
Thank you. I was really worried about how I would pay for my portion.
— Hey, if I hadn't scared you …
Eighty thousand and he was taking the blame? **Still, it wasn't your fault.**
— It's all good.
Mandy stared at the screen. How should she answer that? She sent a smiley emoji.

No more messages came. Just as well. She slipped the phone

onto the desk and returned to her project. She needed to finish the base restoration work before she moved on to the "could be" versions. Halfway through the roof restoration, her phone rang. She looked at the screen, her stylus slipping from her fingers. She hit Control+Z to undo the damage while answering her phone.

ten

"DANIEL?" MANDY HEARD MUFFLED VOICES in the background. She stood and started pacing—almost. Stupid crutches.

"I'll be back in town on Friday. Can I take you to dinner?"

In town? Where was he now? "You have already done enough. You don't need to take me to dinner."

"I want to."

Mandy hopped over to the bed and sank down on it, glad Daniel couldn't see the burning cheeks she could see in her mirror. "Yes. Friday, I am free."

"I'll text you the details. They called my flight. Bye, Amanda."

She stared as the screen turned from green to orange. "Amanda." She hadn't noticed what he called her the other night, but painkillers could be blamed. He used to call her Amanda, saying his name was Daniel, not Danny, and she should go by her proper name too. Apart from a few teachers, Grandma Mae when she was in trouble, and the IRS, no one else ever called her by her given name.

She opened her browser and searched for Daniel Crawford. She raised her eyebrows at the number of fangirl groups she found. He had been sighted at the Chicago airport boarding a flight to London. Who took a two-day trip to London?

A half hour later she got up from her computer. What was she doing reading about his life like some crazed stalker fan? This was just Danny. The boy who didn't know how to skip rocks or climb trees. Yes, he was wealthy, but according to C & O's annual reports, he was working for every penny and was a smart businessman. Dumb with women, though. The only thing she found to recommend Summerset Vandemark was her father's money, and Daniel didn't need that. Why had he dated her for almost two years? One fangirl site speculated DC had dumped Miss Vandemark and that the breakup had been the catalyst for the EMT/Paparazzi fiasco before New Year's. DC had been seen with various women at events, but Summerset maintained they "remained close but had chosen to check out the options before making a further commitment." Mandy returned her focus to the screen and wondered if she could find out more.

What was wrong with her? A tiny reaction to his hands on her waist and she was drooling like the rest of the world. She leaned over and tapped the screen, closing the search.

Daniel settled into his seat. Window—his preference on red-eye flights. Bonnie was good. He hated to lose her. But whether he married or not this year, she deserved to retire.

He opened his phone. Should he text Mandy now?

A coded text from Colin interrupted his musing. **Found things about IN offer you flagged. Look on L's S in locked file.**

How much do I need to worry? Daniel entered the question that would give him the password to the locked file Colin had stored on the London server.

5. Did you get M a birthday gift?

Five and Mandy's birthday, February 9. Now to establish the three letters. **Gave her a Nikon.**

K

Daniel switched his phone to airplane mode. Whatever Colin had found, it was big. Big enough to resort to talking in code. He wondered what he would find when he typed 5M209Nik into the second password box in the London office's secure server tomorrow and why Colin chose Mandy's birthday as the number for the code.

When the flight attendant announced the closing of the plane's doors, Daniel turned off the overhead light, hoping to get some sleep.

eleven

NEXT TO BONNIE, TERRANCE WAS the most efficient office employee in the company. The combination of Terrance's accent and relaxed demeanor soothed Daniel's nerves, allowing him to relax as they drove away from Heathrow.

"I took the liberty of having one of your suits brought round to the office to save you time by not stopping at the flat. Sadly, the tie they delivered was that ghastly yellow one I told you to toss on your last visit. I sent a lad to pick a new one up from Harrods. Don't worry. I ordered it online. You never know when someone is colorblind."

Daniel reclined in his seat. "Thank you. Anything else I should know?"

"Your schedule is sorted out for the day, and I have someone working on an earlier flight. But I think it is unlikely you can leave Thursday evening as the schedule is too tight, and this other firm has a better pitch for you."

Daniel nodded.

The driver stopped at a restaurant. Terrance excused himself and soon returned with a box with steam escaping from its sides. He handed the food to Daniel. "Not quite a proper breakfast, but it will do."

The day's meetings had gone better than anticipated. No groveling on the part of the ad agency. And he met with the vice president of the European branch to discuss branding of a new line of Venetian bakery–inspired desserts in the mid-class restaurants. Daniel logged into the server and the locked file.

Then he picked up the secure phone line and dialed Colin's number. "What exactly am I looking at?"

"The first map is from an Indiana government geological survey of known oil and gas locations. The second is the purchases of the last three years by the conglomerate who owns the real-estate investment firm trying to get your property with the odd mineral-rights clause. The third is from a survey your grandfather commissioned."

"None of these seem important enough to have taken these security measures."

"Have you read the file labeled 'Read me first'?"

"No one ever reads the read-me files." Daniel clicked and did just that. "You're saying either someone got lucky or we have a leak?"

"I don't believe in coincidences. If the 1974 survey is correct, the mineral rights are worth millions. Someone had to know about your grandfather's survey. The Indiana one doesn't show natural gas on your estate, only at a smaller location about twenty miles west."

Daniel clicked through the maps. "Well, now we know why they are so aggressive. I remember seeing a few natural gas wells west of Fort Worth. They resembled mini water tanks. Some were quite discreet. It might be worth exploring the impact of a couple of wells like that, but the pond needs to stay."

Daniel clicked on each surrounding property to bring up the sale information. "Colin, can you ask someone to run a deed check on the ten-acre strip on the south side? Back to 1850, if possible. There was something in the family papers about it, but I don't remember now. It's been years since I paid attention to anything other than the date I can finally sell the land. That little strip was the first parcel sold to the conglomerate and the only one with that type of price per acre. Everyone else sold out for high-end agricultural prices."

"The one sold by a George Fowler? Any relation to Mandy?"

"Uncle. That is where Mandy's grandmother lived, and I am quite sure she has no idea the land sold for 3.4 mil."

Colin gave a low whistle. "Family feuds have been fought over less."

"Go ahead and arrange security personnel to move into the care-taker's house. I can only be there a couple more days this month, and I don't want more surveyors sneaking around. I suspect they are from the big-box store that wants the land for a distribution center, but if they are from the gas company, that changes things."

"Do you know what you are going to do with the place yet?"

"Not a clue."

twelve

MANDY CALLED CANDACE INTO THE bedroom. "Which of these outfits do you think I should wear tonight?"

"Going out?" Candace rubbed a towel over her bald head. "Who is the lucky guy? Please, not the handsy coach."

"Definitely not him." Mandy held up a yellow silk blouse.

"Then who?"

"Daniel."

Candace let out a little scream. "When did he ask you?"

"Tuesday night."

Candace pulled a blue skirt out of Mandy's hand. "Whoa, you got asked out by one of the most eligible bachelors in the world and you didn't tell me? For three whole days? I thought we were friends! And I even did your laundry." She tossed the skirt on the bed and turned to leave.

Mandy caught the sleeve of Candace's robe. "Which is why I have clean choices, thank you. Even if you won't tell me what he wrote."

"Tell me more about this date or I'll go erase it." The green T Candace picked up was quickly discarded.

"I thought it was a joke, but he texted this morning from London and said he would be here at six thirty. And I've got nothing to wear!"

"And only a half hour. Girl, what were you thinking?" Candace dug through the pile on the bed and pulled out a floral miniskirt.

"Too short. I'll end up tugging on it all evening."

"But your legs are fantastic! Even with the boot."

"That is not the type of message I want to send. We are old friends, remember?" Mandy tossed the skirt aside and pulled out a long black one.

"Old friends, not old lady." Candace studied the remaining clothes in the closet before reaching to the back and pulling out a thrift-store find from last year.

"You have never worn this one." She held out the vintage pink-and-white '50s dress complete with netted slip.

"But it's pink." Mandy picked back up the yellow blouse.

"Aren't you the one who told me that according to color theory, pink is the color that makes guys feel most comfortable and therefore attracted to the female wearing it?"

"Yes, which is why I shouldn't wear it."

"That is exactly why you should. Hurry up. We have enough time to do your hair something à la Debbie Reynolds." Candace reached for Mandy's long ponytail.

"But I haven't showered!"

"You did this morning. Use face wipes. Hurry! I have a masterpiece to create."

Mandy hopped into the bathroom as Candace brought up a search for Debbie Reynolds. "Don't get your hair wet!"

Fifteen minutes later, Candace was forcing yet another bobby pin into Mandy's hair. Mandy's cell phone rang, interrupting them. Daniel's number flashed across the screen.

"Hello?"

"Amanda, I'm sorry about this, but my flight got grounded due to the storm. I'm stuck in Minneapolis. Can we take a rain check?"

"Sure." Mandy started pulling out the bobby pins.

"Would tomorrow work for an early dinner, around four? I need to get back to Chicago that night."

Mandy didn't want to seem like she had no social life, but she also didn't want to put off the date any longer. "It works."

"I'm sorry. I couldn't call earlier."

Mandy caught herself worrying her lip in the mirror. "Don't worry about it. Things happen. And being grounded at the wrong airport is the best cancelation excuse I have ever had." She tried to infuse her voice with laughter.

Candace slumped on the bed.

"See you tomorrow."

Mandy set the phone on the nightstand, then stood to unzip the side zipper of the dress.

"He isn't coming, is he." Candace started gathering the bobby pins.

Mandy shrugged. "I knew it wouldn't happen."

"But he made a date for tomorrow, right?"

Mandy hung the dress back in the closet. "It probably won't happen either." She hoped Candace didn't see her swipe at an unwelcome tear. It wasn't as if she had been looking forward to the date. Had she? She pulled on a terry robe and started rehanging the mass of clothes now littering her bed.

"I'd stay and eat some ice cream with you, but my date will be here in a half hour. I'm thinking raven tresses this time. He didn't say a word about the red on Tuesday."

"Wow, three times with the law student."

Candace picked her towel up off the floor. "No, only two. The first was a group thing I went to with one of the girls from the studio."

"So, is he polite or color blind?" Mandy shook out the yellow silk blouse.

"Not sure. I could arrange to lose my wig when he kisses me."

Mandy sucked in a breath. "That is mean, and you know it. That accountant is probably still traumatized."

They burst into laughter. Mandy had come home to find Candace and her accountant mid-kiss. He ended it so abruptly he'd stepped away with his hands still buried in one of the longer haired wigs, revealing Candace in all her bowling-ball glory.

Candace caught her breath. "It wouldn't have been bad, but his frat ring was caught, and he couldn't get the wig off. 'Hi-yah! Hi-yah!'" She mimicked him trying to fling it off his hand.

"Stop it." Mandy sunk onto the bed, holding her sides. "I'm going to pee my pants."

"When it hit him in the face, he screamed like a girl!" Candace threw her arms up and ran from the room. "Made you laugh!" she yelled from down the hall.

Still laughing, Mandy hopped to the bathroom. Grandma Mae called it the curse of the weak bladder. Looking in the mirror, she wiped the tears from her eyes and wondered how many of them were from laughter.

thirteen

DANIEL PULLED A CHAIR OUT for Mandy before taking his seat. He took her crutches and laid them on the floor by the wall. She should have worn pink so at least one of them felt comfortable. The yellow blouse and navy skirt still screamed business meeting even after Candace had added one of her scarfs. A bright flash to her left caught her eye.

Daniel handed her a menu. "Just don't pay attention to them." His voice low enough she wondered if he had spoken. Then, louder, he said, "The chef here studied in Ireland. If you can find a way to work one of his blueberry lemon scones into your choice, you won't be disappointed."

"Scones, as in the British-tea type?"

"His scones make me want to give up coffee for Earl Gray." Daniel's eyes crinkled at the corners.

Another flash, this time from a table behind her. Voices murmured. Mandy caught her name and stiffened. Daniel tapped her leg lightly with his toe. "You okay?"

Mandy shook her head, then nodded. "I mean, I am fine. Just not used to the attention."

"We could order something to go. I tend to forget how uncomfortable eating with people watching you can be."

"I think leaving would cause more of a stir, don't you? I'll make sure not to order anything difficult to eat, like spaghetti." Mandy pretended to read her menu while her heartbeat slowed.

"Sorry, I should have driven farther or opted for fast food." Daniel offered a tentative smile.

"Do you ever get used to it?"

"It is kind of like a zit. If you pick at it, it becomes more noticeable, but if you ignore it, it goes away."

Mandy laughed. "That has got to be the worst analogy I have ever heard!"

"It is what my lawyer told me when I was fifteen."

"Your lawyer?"

"My lawyer, guardian, and foster father, Mr. Thomas Morgan. Not sure what to call him, but he was the one in charge of me after my grandfather and father were killed in the accident. Most of his advice has been very helpful. He is semiretired now, but still makes his presence known in my life almost daily."

"And the zit analogy helped?"

Daniel gave a half smile. "Not really, but when I pictured the paparazzi as big zits waiting to be popped, it kept me from getting mad."

"Ew."

"Hey, I was fifteen." He raised his hands in mock surrender.

Another flash, this time over Daniel's shoulder.

"You know, people need to learn to turn off their flash if they want to take clandestine selfies." Daniel's comment was too loud to be directed at her. Just beyond him, a teenage girl tripped on her way back to her table, her face a deep red.

Mandy frowned. "You realize she will be scarred for life?"

"Not likely. By the time our waiter comes, she will have uploaded the photo to three different sites and declared that DC talked about her." He took a sip of water and settled back in his seat.

Mandy watched the girl tapping on her phone at a speed few of her students could match. Instead of giving him the satisfaction of knowing he was right about it, she set down the menu. "I think I'll have the herb-crusted salmon."

"Good choice."

Once the waiter had taken their orders, Mandy started the conversation. "It probably isn't any of my business, but I have been curious. What does one do in London for two days?"

"Sit in stale-smelling boardrooms with a bunch of stuffy people and negotiate contracts to advertise our restaurant chains."

"I thought C & O was in steel, not food."

"We've diversified over the years. My mother started the restaurants before I was born. She ran them as a separate company. After she—well, it made more sense to bring them under the same umbrella. I spend most of my time on that part of the business. In fact, most of the steel portion has been sold off over the last decade." The half smile again.

A hand clamped down on Mandy's shoulder. Mandy didn't need to look to know it was Coach Robb. "Well, Mandy, I see you managed to make time in your busy schedule to leave your computer."

Mandy tried to brush the hand off her shoulder. She opened her mouth to respond, but Daniel's voice filled the space. "I believe Miss Fowler is uncomfortable with your manhandling. You should return to your table."

Coach Robb never retreated—on the field or off. Mandy tried again to remove his hand as she made introductions. "Coach Robb, this is Daniel Crawford."

"You only go for the rich, nerdy type? Don't know what you are missing." The hand squeezed her shoulder before its owner stalked off.

"Sorry about that." Mandy grimaced as she lifted her glass to her mouth.

"Boyfriend?"

Mandy nearly spewed the sip of water she'd just taken. "Only in his imagination, along with every other woman he sees."

"He asked you out for tonight?"

"Not specifically. His invitation was more open-ended."

Daniel's eyebrows asked the question for him.

Mandy knew she should explain further. "He has been trying to get me to go out with him for a while."

The delivery of their salads saved her from further comment.

Daniel picked up his fork. "You know he is still glaring at me. You sure there is nothing I need to know about?"

Unable to speak because of the bite of avocado in her mouth, Mandy shook her head. Daniel waited.

It had to be the chewiest avocado on earth. Mandy contemplated her answers. Telling him that Candace called the coach "Mr. Handsy" probably wouldn't go over well. "Let's say I actively avoid him as the words 'not interested' don't seem to be in his vocabulary. I am sure you have met a few people like that." Another cell phone flashed, as if to punctuate her sentence.

"Touché." Daniel saluted her with a forkful of salad. "I may have met one or two thousand like him?"

"Only two thousand?"

A tinge of a blush colored his cheeks.

Teasing him was as easy as it had been twenty years ago. "I'm sure if they knew how adorable you were in Hulk swim trunks and with mud on your face, you would have to double that."

Daniel gave a fake shudder. "I should have never let you talk me into those. I wanted the Spiderman ones."

"But, as Grandma Mae told you, they were not on sale."

The smile slid from Daniel's face. "When did she pass?"

"Four years ago, near the end of my student teaching. I came home, and she was sitting in the rocker like she did every afternoon—only she wasn't rocking." Mandy waved a hand in front of her face, trying to fan away the moisture that had started to gather in her eyes.

"You were living with her?"

"Yes, she didn't want to move to a retirement home or down with my parents. So I chose to come to school up here."

"I tried to drive by her house the other day and couldn't find it."

"Tornado." Mandy stuffed a bite of roll in her mouth to give herself some time to keep the tears at bay.

"Three years ago, right? I think I had every roofing company in the state calling me for months."

She jumped on the new subject. "Why didn't you get the roof fixed? From the photos I took, it looks like you may have some water damage."

Daniel studied the tomato on his fork. "I assure you, repairs were made. I just didn't replace the roof. I was kind of mad the tornado wasn't a few hundred yards northwest."

"You wanted it to destroy the mansion?"

Daniel steered away from answering that question. "Were you in the house?"

"No, I had already moved into town. Grandma Mae told me I would inherit the house but must have never informed her lawyer. Uncle George let me stay until the end of the semester and graduation. He was trying to sell the property, so the house was vacant when the tornado hit. Grandma's was the only house destroyed in that tornado as it hit so far north of town."

"It did take out most of the back fence, as I recall, as well as the archway and main gate."

"Yes, you had no problem fixing that." *With a hideous chain link fence.* Mandy hoped the bitterness she felt was not evident. How could he have neglected fixing the mansion? Boarding up windows did not constitute a fix in her book. Didn't he know how rare a late-nineteenth-century home was in this part of the country?

Daniel opened his mouth to reply, but the waiter chose that moment to deliver their entrees.

He picked up his fork. "You loved that house, didn't you?"

"Grandma Mae's? Yes, but I love the memories more—working in her garden, watching stars from the gable room."

"Don't forget the Morse code window." Daniel bit into his steak. The book in his grandfather's library had been most helpful. At first they had used the lights in their bedrooms to communicate, but switching the light on and off fast blew Grandma Mae's breaker, so Daniel acquired a pair of heavy-duty flashlights.

Daniel tapped his knife on the table. "Dash-dash-dot, dash-dot." G-N—their code for "good night."

"Dash-dot, dash-dot-dash-dash," Mandy tapped back.

"N-Y. Not yet? You never did want to stop."

Mandy shook her head. "I couldn't stop if I didn't think you were happy."

"What do you mean?"

Too late Mandy realized what she would have to reveal. "You needed to go to sleep happy so you wouldn't cry, or your grandfather wouldn't let me play with you."

"How did you know that?"

"The first time Grandma Mae took me over to the mansion, I met your grandfather. He said I could only play with you if it kept you from crying at night. Scared me to death."

Daniel set down his utensils. "You never said anything about that."

"Grandma Mae told me it should be a secret because big boys didn't like to cry and asked me to do my best to make you smile."

"Did she tell you why I cried?"

Mandy shook her head. "She said it was your secret and when you wanted to tell me, you would, and I was never to ask. I think Grandma Mae repeated that almost every day before I climbed the fence."

Daniel shook his head. "You must have asked me every other question in the universe that summer, but you never asked that one. Do you know the answer yet?"

"That summer your mother died. Wikipedia solved that one for me a while ago."

"You looked me up?"

"Hasn't every woman over the age of ten?" Mandy wanted to return to their teasing.

"Why?"

She hid behind her napkin for a moment, wiping an imaginary crumb. "Because I wanted to figure out if Mr. Most Eligible was the boy I caught frogs with."

"One and the same."

"Are you sure?"

fourteen

As soon as the question left her lips, she knew she shouldn't have asked it. Daniel didn't answer. Mandy took another bite of her fish, which seemed to be composed of bones as she tried to swallow.

"Sorry, that was rude of me," she squeaked out.

Daniel set his fork down. "No, you're right. I've become jaded. And suspicious. As I have proven." He gestured to the crutches. "I am sorry."

"You don't need to keep apologizing. Why did you think I was a land developer?" She ignored the flash of another camera.

"About a year ago I started looking at options. I have at least six offers on the land I have been sitting on, waiting for Grandfather's stipulations to expire so I can sell. A couple of the buyers are getting desperate, sending surveyors, photographers, etc."

"Why would you want to sell your home?"

"It never really was mine. I lived there until I was two, but I don't remember it. Spent a few Christmases there as a child and one very memorable summer. After my mother died, my father and I only went back a few times. To me the mansion was my grandfather's home, never mine."

"Surely you don't want to destroy it. Architecturally it is a perfect example of Victorian Gothic revival. I am surprised it isn't on the National Registry."

Daniel made a face. "Grandfather was adamant about that. Didn't want some government park official telling him he couldn't paint the place purple if he wanted to."

"Purple? Like the house out on Spring Creek? If you did, I would trespass just to paint it period colors."

"If you did, I wouldn't yell or be rude." Daniel's voice took on a somber tone.

Mandy wanted to return to a lighter subject but she couldn't figure out how. "Did you know they almost called in the bomb squad over the camera delivery?"

"Really? Why?"

"Your private carrier bypassed central receiving and delivered an anonymous box straight to the dean's secretary. I am glad they didn't try to detonate it."

He flashed the same smile that graced every fangirl's pin board. "Oh, I didn't know it would cause trouble."

"Don't worry about it. Dr. Christensen, my adviser, is still laughing about everyone running around like Armageddon was in the box. Says it's the most life that has been in the college all year. The dean is happy to have a replacement camera with little effort. And I'm glad to be able to graduate. Having an MFA gives me a few more options than teaching high school for the rest of my life."

"Don't you like teaching?"

Mandy swallowed her bite of asparagus. "I love teaching the students who want to learn, but many of my students are trying to get an easy A or just filling hours. They don't want to be there and make no attempt to hide it. Then their parents call me when they get a C."

The waiter approached. Daniel ordered a double batch of the scones to go.

After the waiter left, Mandy asked, "Why to-go?"

"We seem to have garnered more than the local cell-phone paparazzi. The photographer who just stuck his head into the lobby looks like a pro. We will be leaving through the kitchen if Geoff will let us."

The waiter delivered their boxed scones, and Daniel handed him three bills with smiling Ben Franklins on them. After retrieving the crutches, he helped Mandy out of her chair and whispered, "Pretend you are going to the restroom, then slip into the kitchen. I'll be there in a moment."

The waiter held open the kitchen door and gave Mandy a little nod. Daniel entered before she needed to say anything. Without a word, he motioned her to follow. They passed a short man dressed in white, Daniel nodded and held up his box. Now Mandy understood Daniel's choice of parking space —better than to have to walk around the building if a quick exit became necessary. As he opened the door and swept her into the cab, a man ran around the side of the building, a camera dangling from his neck, another from his hand. Before he got into position, Daniel had the truck out of the parking space.

Mandy held on to the door handle as the truck turned the corner faster than she liked.

After several minutes of driving, Daniel stopped looking in the rearview mirror as often as he looked forward. "Sorry about that. I had hoped they would leave me alone tonight. Usually when I am down this way I can get by relatively unnoticed. But this was the first time I have been on a date in the area, and I guess someone decided it would be newsworthy."

"Usually when you're down here? How often are you here?"

"I spend a week or so every few months here, but I keep a low profile. It has only been since that stupid magazine article that the locals have noticed me."

"That explains how you know more about the area restaurants than I do."

Daniel turned down a tiny lane, stopping at a familiar gate.

Mandy looked around in confusion, but she would recognize the old walnut tree anywhere. The Crawford Manson.

Mandy's unasked question hung in the cab of the truck while Daniel unlocked the gate. He should have gone around to the gate with the automatic opener. He wouldn't lie if she asked, but he wasn't ready to show her where he was living just yet.

"I thought the pond would be a nice place to share our scones, no trespassers allowed you know." He drove around the house toward the west side of the property where the fading sun cast a warm glow over the unkempt lawn. He stopped his truck as close to the pond as he could. They would still need to hike a few dozen yards. Her boot—how could he have forgotten?

"Do you think you and your boot can make the hike?"

Mandy pulled her gaze from the window. "Just you try to stop me." She opened her door and moved to slide out, but Daniel caught her wrist. "Please wait." Mandy leaned back against the seat.

Before going around to get her, he pulled a flashlight and blanket from behind the seat, then set them on the hood. He should have driven the Lexus because it would be easier for her to get in and out, but that would mean losing the few moments of contact helping her out of the truck permitted.

Mandy cleared her throat once he'd lifted her down, and Daniel relinquished his hold and handed her the crutches. He gathered the blanket and flashlight in one arm.

They had only gone a few steps when Mandy stopped. "The scones!"

Daniel turned back to the truck.

By the time he returned to her side, she had moved several yards down the path. He started to reach for her hand but pulled back. Crutches were not ideal for romance. The last rays of sunshine sparkled off the water. The ducks honked their protests at the invaders, but no doubt they would search for handouts later.

Mandy stopped. "It hasn't changed much, has it? I used to come here every summer hoping you would come back, but you never did."

"Every summer?"

"Until I was thirteen or so. I stopped after I saw you in the news—in the procession at your father and grandfather's funeral. I knew even if you came back, you wouldn't want to fly kites, so I stopped looking."

"So, Miss I-Wasn't-Trespassing, you are telling me you trespassed every summer for the next six—"

"Seven."

"—seven years?" They'd reached the edge of the pond, and Daniel spread out the blanket.

"I wasn't exactly trespassing. The old gardener would wave to me. And one year I was sure he took the pole out of the fence so I could get in."

"Just how often did you come?"

"The first year, I came every day for weeks until I believed Grandma Mae that you were not living here."

"I was in Tokyo with my father." Daniel offered Mandy a hand to help her sit down on the blanket. It took her a couple of tries to find a way to sit gracefully in her tight skirt. More evidence this was not one of his well-thought-out plans. "Sorry. I should have thought ahead better. But I love this spot. It's the reason I am having such a hard time deciding on a buyer. Most of the options will end up destroying this section."

"Perhaps you shouldn't sell." Mandy smiled up at him and patted the blanket next to her. "I want to try one of those scones before the ducks realize we have them."

"Are you still scared of ducks?" He recalled her six-year-old self, sopping wet and screaming for help. *"They are going to kill me! Save me! Save me!"* Of course he had. He didn't need to be

Hulk to scare them off, but he had carried her away from the pond with superhero-like strength.

Mandy interrupted his musings. "No, but I don't want them to eat what is mine, either."

He watched as she took her first bite. Her eyes closed like they did whenever she had eaten one of Cook's special peanut-butter cookies.

"Oh, these are good. Had I known, I would have skipped the salmon entirely." She held her hand in front of her mouth to hide the fact that she was still eating.

They ate the scones and shooed the ducks away when they came too close.

Mandy finished the last of her scones. "You would think after all these years they would get weary of humans. They can't be the same ducks, can they?"

Daniel shook his head. "The average wild mallard only lives five to ten years. So these are grandchildren or great-grandchildren."

"Good. I would hate it if Hank recognized me."

"You never know—he might have passed on the story of the girl who tried to steal his sandwich."

"You have that backward. He stole my sandwich. Do you still speak duck?"

Daniel laughed. "Not a single quack." He'd felt silly lecturing the ducks in their language, but his act had made Mandy laugh and the frightened tears go away before she'd hugged him and given him a kiss on the cheek for saving her life. He hadn't appreciated a kiss then.

"Too bad. I would ask you to tell them there are no more scones." Her eyes grew wide, and she leaned toward him and plucked something off the front of his shirt. "Except for this one." She popped the large crumb into her mouth before he could get it back.

"Hey, that isn't fair!"

Mandy shook her head. "Finders keepers."

"Really?"

Mandy nodded.

"If I find a crumb?" He gave a crooked smile.

Mandy studied her clothing before answering. "All yours."

Mandy stilled when he reached out and cupped her jaw. "There is one on the corner of your mouth." He could have easily wiped it off with his thumb, and he had meant to at first, but Mandy's eyes fluttered closed, so he kissed her—a soft brush to dislodge the crumb and let her protest. A second brush to be sure she wouldn't pull back, then a kiss. It was evident she wasn't as experienced as the women he'd kissed these last several years. He deepened the kiss when she responded like a butterfly—soft, fragile, beautiful. Her hand on his chest rested lightly, not pulling him in but not pushing him away either. Not wanting to push her too far, he pulled back.

Mandy blinked at him. "Is it gone?"

Daniel studied her face in the dimming light. The weariness in her eyes told him she had yet to decide if she needed her fight or flight response. The crumb rested near her chin, so he lied. "No more crumbs."

"Good, I would hate for Hank's great-grandson to see a crumb there."

I would too, darling. "Don't worry. I would save you."

Mandy leaned against his shoulder and watched the pond.

fifteen

PART OF MANDY WONDERED EXACTLY what number she was on DC's list. In the past few years, she had replaced Candace's three-date rule with her own ten-date law. No one ever stayed around long. She longed to tell Daniel she wasn't that kind of girl.

She shivered.

His arm came around her. "We don't have jackets. I think I should take you home. I need to get back to Chicago. I fly to New York in the morning for the paparazzi and Vandemark trials."

"I've read about them." Mandy didn't want to think about the gorgeous socialite Daniel had dated for more than a year. "Do you have to be there for both trials?"

"Unfortunately. I hope they can be resolved quickly."

A lone duck swam across the pond, its quacking answered from the far bank.

"Whatever you do, please promise to leave this pond here." She would have asked for more, but shared memories of a single summer gave her little right.

Daniel nodded against Mandy's head and pulled her closer.

Neither of them moved for several minutes. Mandy wished the fireflies were out. It would be an excuse to sit there longer.

When Hank's great-grandson quacked, breaking the silence, Mandy forced herself to shift away from Daniel's side. He stood and helped her to her feet. For a second she thought he would kiss her again, but he stepped back and grabbed the crutches.

He handed her the flashlight. "Can you turn it on?"

Holding the light awkwardly against her crutch, Mandy kept it aimed at the ground to not blind either of them and hopped off the blanket.

Daniel shook the blanket and folded it in half before wrapping it around her shoulders. "You're still shivering." He took the flashlight from her hand. Mandy tucked the blanket more tightly around herself to prevent it from sliding as she maneuvered on her crutches. Daniel guided her to the truck.

Mandy wondered if her shivering had more to do with the man than it did the dropping temperatures. Several yards from the truck, Daniel stopped and turned off the flashlight. He stepped into her space, set his hands on her waist, pulled her close, then rested his chin on her head for a moment before he spoke. "Amanda, I am not going to say I am sorry for the kiss, because I am not."

Mandy felt the *but* hanging in the air.

"But I am sorry for the timing. I have some things I committed to attend to in New York with various women. Some of it is for publicity, and I can't explain more. I don't want you to think I am using you or—" He let the sentence hang.

"Do you usually kiss on the first date?" Mandy would have covered her mouth, but Daniel stood too close.

"Regardless of what the tabloids say, or will say, I am not a player. Back when I was at college, maybe, but not as bad as I might have been. Mr. Morgan saw to that." He paused to lift his face to the stars. "But no, I don't normally kiss on the first date, and I suspect you don't either."

Mandy hoped that didn't call for an answer.

"But if we stand here much longer, I will probably kiss you again, and I don't know if that is wise."

She felt him shift away as the flashlight came back to life. No, it wouldn't be wise at all.

Stupid.

Double stupid.

Wonderful.

Daniel turned on the radio, hoping to find something to distract his thoughts during the nearly three-hour drive to Chicago. Love song, love ballad, polka music. Seriously?

Mandy was not some Hollywood A-lister who had grown immune to the power of a kiss, or a socialite who expected such was her due. At dinner, he'd admitted to becoming jaded, but when he kissed her tonight, he realized it was more than that. He had forgotten what real felt like.

And real was a dangerous thing. Especially when the next two weeks required he act as if he were vying for an Oscar. Why had he agreed to his legal team's plan? At the time, the high-profile social life seemed like a good idea. But that was before Amanda had fallen back into his life. The worst part was, he couldn't explain why he was going to spend as much time trying to get in the gossip columns as he would be sitting in the courtroom.

Not only had the DA subpoenaed his testimony for the criminal trial of the paparazzi, but Summerset's lawyers'—or her father's— had planned the civil suit against the hotel to coincide with the state's prosecution of the paparazzi. It was a media frenzy in the making, and he had managed to land himself in the middle of it, as vulnerable as a bleeding diver in a shark cage.

The tones of his phone interrupted his thoughts. He answered using the car's hands-free feature.

Thomas Morgan skipped any formalities. "Couldn't you wait two more weeks? What is wrong with you?"

I'm not sure, but I think you are going to tell me. "What are you talking about, Morgan?"

"A date in Podunk, Indiana? They have cell phones there too! How many times must I tell you citizens with camera phones are ten times worse than the paparazzi? They post their unfiltered opinions. And there are more than a few about the art teacher and the millionaire."

"We only had dinner." Morgan didn't need to know about dessert at the pond.

"I know you. That's not your dinner face. It isn't even your what's-for-dessert face. And don't try to tell me it's just friends. That photo is of a man who is falling hook, line, and sinker. And by their comments, your fans know it too. You are no actor, as you proved last year on that reality whatever-it-was."

Daniel concentrated on keeping his car in the lane. Morgan had to be wrong. "She is an old friend; we were catching up."

Thomas ignored his protest and continued. "PR is having a fit. She doesn't have a contract. Did you hear any part of their "keep to the script until the lawsuit is over" lecture? Never be seen with the same woman twice, only take out women who will mutually benefit from the exposure, and don't get serious. Three months of carefully scheduled dates, and you go impromptu."

"You said this Amanda is an old friend."

"Yes. I met her the summer Grandfather kept me at his mansion." Daniel exited the freeway.

"PR might be able to do something with that, but you had better get her on board. You didn't do something foolish like sleep with her, did you?"

Daniel struggled to keep his voice calm. "She isn't that type of woman."

"Fortunately for you, I believe you. I'm not going to ask for any details, but wherever you were after the restaurant, could some amateur have taken your photo?"

"Not legally."

"You had better hope so. And you make sure she doesn't do an interview."

Daniel glanced at the clock on his dash 10:58, nearly midnight in Amanda's time zone. He'd call her in the morning.

The house had been dark when Daniel dropped her off. She had hoped he might kiss her again on the doorstep, but the lingering hug was almost as good. The silence between them had not been as awkward as it was full of promise.

Too early to go to bed and too restless to work, Mandy headed for the grocery store. The scooter carts were all available. She took one and cruised the nearly empty aisles. Candace had shopped that morning, so other than the tomatoes she had forgotten, Mandy didn't need anything.

She stopped in the frozen-foods aisle. What would Candace think? They were years beyond the tradition, but a carton of mint chocolate chip would lead to a conversation. She was back in first-kiss territory and needed advice.

Only two checkout lines were open. Mandy steered the cart to the one closest to the door. Ahead of her, a teenage girl was bent over her phone, tapping her feet to a tune only she could hear through hot-pink earbuds. The customer in front of them left, and the girl moved up.

The scooter jerked and banged into the end of the checkout stand as Mandy tried to move close enough to deposit her purchases on the conveyor belt.

The girl spun around, her glare fading. "Miss Fowler! Is it true?"

Mandy couldn't place the teen beyond seeing her in the hallways of the high school. "Is what true?"

The girl extended her phone. A photo of Mandy and Daniel at the restaurant filled the screen. Mandy squinted to try to make out the writing but failed.

"Wow, it's true! You are wearing the same blouse. Is your date over already? That was quick. Is he as hot in person? Oh, ice cream—did he dump you already? I'm not surprised. Slumming it with a high school teacher. Not like you are DC's type."

Mandy felt the heat rising in her face.

The girl's fingers flew over the face of her phone. Then she turned and snapped a picture.

"Excuse me? What are you doing?" Mandy tried to keep her voice steady. Ramming the cart into the presumptuous teen was tempting.

"They're going to be so excited I saw you!"

Shoppers turned their direction. The girl answered the cashier. Mandy cursed the boot on her foot. If she wasn't on the scooter, she would abandon the food on the conveyor belt. The girl paid the cashier, turned her back to Mandy, and raised her arm to take a selfie.

At the slightest touch, the scooter jerked toward the girl, who jumped away. "Hey, you ruined my picture."

"Oh, pardon me." Mandy used her teacher's voice. "I was just trying to check out." She smiled sweetly and turned her attention to the cashier, ignoring the curses coming from the teen.

Mandy returned the cart to its place near the exit and hobbled toward her car, her bag banging against the crutches. The now-angry girl moved to block her. "I still need a photo."

Mandy ducked her head and tried to move around her. Daniel's advice about the paparazzi being a zit came to mind. She pictured the teen with a large one in the center of her forehead and nearly laughed out loud.

Once again, the girl moved to block her.

Only two more car lengths to her little Golf. Mandy turned between two cars, forcing the girl to run around them, then zigzagged through the cars to reach hers before the girl had a chance to get a picture.

Pulling out of the lot, Mandy hoped the girl had a warehouse-sized supply of face cream for all the zits.

sixteen

CANDACE SCOOPED THE LAST OF the mint ice cream into a bowl. "Best breakfast ever. I still can't believe you kissed him."

Mandy's face burned anew. She'd spent all night agonizing over the kiss. Why her? Stupidly she'd searched for photos of Daniel with his old flames and analyzed the kisses. And the women. The girl at the store last night was right—a ponytailed-vintage-clothes-wearing high school teacher was slumming it. Mandy would never be as thin or as fashionable as any of those women. "I should have never bought the ice cream. Your advice has been less than helpful." *I want to know I am not a number.*

"I thought my idea was quite original. Starting a 'Have you kissed DC?' website is brilliant. Think of the ad revenue."

"No way am I becoming another fangirl. I already feel like a number. Why would I want to know which one?" Mandy eyed her phone. She would not check for a text. The phone vibrated, causing her to jump. She reached for it to the sound of Candace's laughter.

"Careful, or you'll choke on that ice cream." Mandy warned, opening her phone.

Morning. Sleep well?

Sleep? Not exactly. **Well enough. How was your drive?** No way did she want to know how he'd slept.

— Long. May I call?
Sure.

Mandy took her phone with the intention of hiding in her room. Slowed by her crutches, she was closer to the library when the phone rang, she sunk into one of the chairs.

"I wanted to let you know how sorry I am."

"Sorry?" Candace's speculations still on her mind, Mandy knew he would end up apologizing for the kiss. She wasn't the type of girl he frequently dated.

"For taking you out in public. I shouldn't have asked—"

As she'd expected, she wasn't thin enough, pretty enough, or rich enough. Hurt coursed through her veins. "I'm sorry if I embarrassed you."

"That isn't what I—"

Mandy used the calm voice she reserved for her third-hour students, all the doubts of her sleepless night tumbled out. "I think you've made it clear. Congratulations on adding another name to your list of conquests. Did you need the 'girl next door' to complete your bingo card? In New York, with any luck you can add an A-lister and an heiress."

"Please, listen. That's not—"

Tears filled her eyes, blurring the screen as she pressed End. The phone rang again.

Mandy hit Ignore and tossed it into the other chair. The stairway to the loft beckoned her. Boot or no boot, it was a good place to hide.

No, Daniel didn't want to leave a message on voicemail. He checked the time. The car service would be here any minute. He growled in frustration.

Amanda—that came out wrong. Please call me back.

He dialed Bonnie.

"This better be good to bother my Sunday, and if this is about your social life, I am out."

"Just making sure you have what you need before I leave for two weeks."

"Liar. You were calling to get me to send flowers to that poor girl. She is no Vandemark, and those vipers will tear her apart. Did you know her photo is plastered all over one of those fan sites, and she is dubbed the newest woman to hate? No, you clean this one up yourself. She deserves more than flowers from a secretary. And don't forget your toothbrush."

The line went dead. For a moment he considered calling Colin, but Colin would probably be even less inclined to help.

Amanda's phone went to voicemail again. He tried a longer text. **I wanted to be out with you. I was talking about the publicity because I took you to a place where people took your photo. I feel like I threw you to the sharks. Please call. Things might get nasty. My friend Colin is a whiz with computers, and he can do some things to help electronically hide you. I didn't mean for this to happen.**

Daniel checked his shaving bag for a toothbrush, even though he hadn't forgotten one in years.

On his way to the airport, he tried Mandy's number again only to be dumped into voicemail. "Mandy, I hope to see you when I get back so we can talk. I was only trying to apologize for dragging you into my world. You deserve some privacy, not a mess that can only get worse. Please call me and please, please, please never trust a tabloid."

Inadequate. He clicked End. Ordering flowers online wasn't going to be much better, but at least it was something. He scrolled through the site, discarding several arrangements, before he came to a light-pink, dark-pink, and lavender rose bouquet, the colors reminding him of the impressionist painting on one of the kitchen cabinets. Roses—not red but colors that spoke of new love and sweetness. One hundred and twenty blooms might be excessive. He pondered for a moment before adding the bouquet to the cart. An option to add a stuffed animal popped up. He didn't think Mandy was a collector, but then a stuffed mallard caught his eye. The message was problematic because in the end the order would go through a local florist and someone was bound to talk. After several tries, he was happy with it.

Sunday delivery was unavailable in such a small town, he selected an option for "as soon as possible" and noted the "Delivery may take up to 72 hours" disclaimer. Not ideal, but he was running out of ideas.

After navigating airport security, he waited in a private lounge. His photo flashed on one of the television screens, followed by one of him talking to Mandy over salad at the restaurant. He couldn't hear the show host, but the banner headline "DC and the Girl Next Door" was loud and clear.

He pulled out his phone. No answer.

Please, Mandy. I need to know you are safe. Some groupies are crazy.

Five minutes later, still no return text. He did a search on his name. The top five stories featured amateur photos of last night's date. *No! Amanda doesn't deserve this.*

He dialed Colin. "I need your help."

Raindrops danced over the skylight, and thunder rolled in the distance. Mandy pulled the fleece blanket tight around her shoulders. The gray clouds matched her mood, only she had no more tears to shed. She needed to go down and work on the images for the mansion. The first one had been completed days ago. The traditional home of the Crawford family was repainted, shutters open, windows gleaming. She added a play gym in the backyard, like Danny had always wished. For a moment she dreamed she had been a part of that scene, supervising the meals, welcoming guests, playing with several dark-haired children in the nursery.

She reminded herself that half the women in the free world had the same dream and that hers was over. She would not be in public, or private, with him again.

She tossed a pillow against the wall like some tantrum-tossing toddler. Sorry he took her out in public? Enough. She needed to focus on the mansion, not its owner. If she was going to have the project done in less than three weeks, she had better start on one of the other ideas. A long-term mental-health facility had certain charm. Mandy scooted to the stairway, chagrined that the best way to get down with her boot on was to slide down.

Her phone chimed with a text as she walked through the library. Wondering if she had been too hasty with Daniel earlier, Mandy retrieved it from the chair. No. Way. It wasn't possible to have 1,438 text messages, was it? No way would any guy text that much.

The icons on the main screen indicated she had even more messages in her social media accounts.

A new message popped up.

He is mine, you little brat.

And another **You go, girl! One for the little people!**

And another, this time a photo from the restaurant with her head distorted like Munch's *The Scream.*

Another message and yet another—the vilest of all. Mandy dropped the phone. "Candace!"

A muffled "Studio!" was her answer. Mandy abandoned her crutches and followed the echo back to the glass-walled room, arms wrapped around her middle. She only took two steps into the studio before Candace wrapped her arms around her. "What is it?"

"My phone." Mandy shuddered. "Over a thousand messages. Calling me names."

Candace's brow knit. "Show me."

Mandy shuffled back to the library.

Candace bent and retrieved the phone. "No way!" Candace pulled out her phone and sunk into one of the chairs. She opened app after app. "Mandy, I think you are going to want to get a new phone number and close your social media accounts. Not only are there photos of your date yesterday, but someone posted your cell number. Have you checked your email?" Candace handed back the phone.

Mandy hit the email icon. Only three messages sat in her inboxes. "Both my work and personal emails seem to be the typical junk."

Candace stood and handed Mandy her crutches. "Shut your phone down, then, and let's see what we can do about your social media accounts."

Airplane mode was a beautiful thing, but coming out of it stunk. Daniel watched his voicemail, text, and email boxes fill up. Had Mandy called?

Colin, Mr. Morgan, Summerset, and Bonnie had all left multiple messages.

Bonnie never left messages on Sunday, and she avoided texting. He read Bonnie's text first. **Give me her contact information before you mess things up any more!** To the point, as usual. Daniel would call her when he got to the hotel.

He skipped Summerset's and Morgan's texts. He would deal with them later. Avoiding Summerset until the trial would be best, though impossible. The crazy rumors she'd started showed how disconnected she had become from reality. The only reason he kept any dialogue with her was on the advice of his legal team.

Colin's text caused Daniel to stop abruptly on the Jetway, the man behind him swearing as a result. Stronger words ran through Daniel's mind as he reread the text.

She has death threats. Call me!

It was tempting to hit speed dial then, but anyone would be able to hear his conversation in the middle of JFK. The car-service vehicle was not the best place for a conversation either.

He squelched the urge to try to hurry the driver through the Sunday-afternoon traffic. The messages on his voicemail did little to calm his nerves. Bonnie's was almost word for word her text, and Summerset's voice was more needy than sultry, but there was no way he was going to eat dinner with her, tonight or any other night. He may be a witness for the prosecution in the legal case, but in her civil case, he was testifying for the defense. Once she realized this, she was going to toss one of her patented billion-dollar-heiress fits. It was best he avoid her altogether.

Colin texted again: **Are you at the hotel yet?**

— Two blocks.

I expect to be your first call, before Bonnie.

Interesting. They must have been conversing.

If he hadn't been preoccupied with his phone when he got out of the car, the next few minutes would have been very different. But he did not hear the high-pitched squeal of "Da-a-rli-i-i-ing!" until the last syllable was far too close to his ear. Daniel looked up in time to be simultaneously blinded by a camera flash and Summerset's lips nearly upon his. A quick move offered only his cheek for the landing. He set her back from him as swiftly as he could.

"Miss Vandemark, I didn't expect you here."

She sidled up to him, forcing him to take a step back. "Didn't you get all my messages?"

The calculated batting of her eyelids curdled his stomach. What had he ever seen in her? He took a sidestep and moved to the door of the hotel. The paparazzi already had too much fodder. Depending on the angle, a photo could tell a thousand lies. He passed the doorman. Behind him, Summerset gave a little squeak. Several curious onlookers suddenly remembered they had something else to do as he approached the desk. Maybe he should consider getting an apartment in Manhattan. Two weeks of this might kill him.

seventeen

DANIEL'S PHONE RANG AS HE shut the door to his suite. Thomas Morgan. Daniel braced for the lecture.

"Congratulations. You set a new record for headlines. Did you have to kiss Miss Vandemark on the sidewalk?"

"I was ambushed." Daniel didn't want to have this conversation.

"Obviously. That is the only way the photos could be up on the web before you finished checking in."

"How bad is everything else?"

"You need to ask Colin. The larger tabloids are only speculating and are being careful not to show her face in any photos. But I am sure they are digging into her background. I think social media is the problem. Did you get a hold of her?"

"She hasn't returned my calls or texts, but Colin's text said something about threats."

"Yes, I took the liberty of having Hastings's security team start to watch her. Call Colin."

Daniel kicked off his shoes and dialed Colin's number.

"About time."

"What is this about threats?" Daniel paced the suite.

"Your fangirls are not happy you dined with the girl next door, and a few of them crossed the line. I put one of my filters on her email service and blocked those, but it's the social media sites I worry about. I was already monitoring her accounts, so I have been reporting the threats to the services as they appear. A couple of hours ago someone posted her phone number. It is down now, but I have no idea what type of texts she has been getting. She must be freaked out. Her phone is currently off, and she has been suspending her social media accounts. I wish she would change her passwords. Far too simple. One of my guys is working on securing her blog. And don't worry, I am paying them all double time since it is Sunday afternoon."

"What type of threats?"

"There have been three death threats and one disfigurement using acid. Mostly there is either nasty name calling or fangirls cheering her on. Her high school email is the most visible. The district's server forces people to register to send emails to teachers or to use a website comment form. It's bounced off several emails today. Nothing out of the ordinary I can see getting through. Her personal email is clean so far. I don't think anyone has discovered it yet."

Daniel completed his tenth circuit of the room. "I should ask you about the legality of your methods, but right now I don't care. Even if you have email addresses I don't."

Colin chuckled.

"Morgan said he was sending some of Hastings's people to watch her. Do you think that's necessary?"

"Definitely. Anyone with half-decent computer skills could locate her or her roommate. Now, *she* is one fascinating woman."

"Colin."

"Sorry. I take it you haven't been able to talk to Mandy."

"I tried this morning, but I said something wrong and she went off and hung up on me. I called, texted, and ordered flowers, but they won't arrive today." Daniel pushed his hands through his hair.

"Idiot." The word was muttered, but it came through as clear as Colin's next sentence. "You need to assume she never got your text or voicemail. The flowers may be your only hope."

"What else can we do?"

"Well, unless she reports the threats herself or something happens, we can't do much. Try an email."

Daniel paced again. "Amanda never gave me an address, and my guess is that if the school's is monitored, I couldn't say much in an email anyway."

"Overnight a letter, but you probably missed the cutoff to have it delivered by tomorrow. You had better call Bonnie."

"I don't wanna." Daniel sunk into a chair

"Be a big boy. She can't ground you, can she?" Colin chuckled and ended the call.

Daniel stared at his phone. The longer he waited, the worse it would be.

"Hello, Bonnie."

Candace leaned over Mandy's shoulder. "Do you think I should suspend my accounts, too? Some of these women are evil."

Mandy shrugged. "Too bad I can't tell them he already dumped me."

"He what?" Candace spun Mandy's desk chair around.

I am not going to cry again. "Daniel called this morning and said he was sorry he ever took me out."

"The nerve. Are you sure that is what he said?"

Mandy nodded, tears forming. Impossible. There was nothing left to cry.

Tapping her chin, Candace brightened. "I've been thinking. I know I have a no-overnight rule, but after reading a couple of those messages, I wonder if we shouldn't call a couple of guys and have them stay here tonight. What about Gordon and his husband? They both have the build to scare someone off, and they won't be distracted by us." Candace gave Mandy a funny smile.

"Hey, I wasn't the one who hit on Gordon, remember?" Mandy gave a half laugh. "Sure, call them."

"You should call Daniel. He made this mess for you."

Mandy pointed to her boot. "You think I would have gotten smart the moment I saw him. Lover's Fracture. I should have been running from him, not falling for him. All he has done is made messes."

"Hey, he did replace the camera, and he took the time to do it personally. Didn't your Grandma Mae say something about time being love?"

"Time isn't money. It is love. Watch where people spend their time, and you will know what they love," Mandy repeated by rote.

"Yup, that. Now call him." Candace handed Mandy her phone.

"I can't. I would have to turn on my phone." The crutch slipped, Mandy bit back a curse. The doctor had said two to three weeks. Tomorrow was close enough to two weeks for her. Part of her life could get easier.

eighteen

MANDY PULLED INTO HER REGULAR parking place behind the school. Three police cars were lined up outside the south entrance. Unusual at any time but especially before school. She glanced at the space near the front of the school where the resource officer usually parked with his K-9 unit. That spot was empty. She shouldered her bag and walked to the side entrance.

The principal, Mr. Lee, stood at the door, talking to one of the officers. He turned his attention to her. "Miss Fowler, I have been trying to reach you. You need to take the day off."

"Sorry, I had a slight problem yesterday and turned off my phone."

The officer stepped into her space. "Miss Fowler, I am Officer Keller. What kind of problems?"

"Just crazy text messages." *Seriously, what business is it of the police?*

"Have you received any threats?" The officer opened a notebook.

Mandy shifted her weight and immediately regretted it, perhaps she should have waited a few more days before abandoning her crutches. "Can I please go to my room? I need to sit down."

"I'm afraid your room was vandalized last night, but perhaps we can take a seat in the ceramics room." Mr. Lee held open the door.

Down the hall, two more officers and some guy who could model for a Marine ad stood outside her classroom.

"Miss Fowler?"

Mandy turned her attention back to the principal, who was holding the back of the rolling teacher's chair for her. The officer pulled up one of the molded plastic student seats. "Now, back to my question. Were any of them threats?"

"I only read a few of the text messages. They mostly called me names. There were close to 1,600 messages when I turned off my phone."

The principal gave a funny half smile. "If this weren't such a serious matter, I would laugh. You may have gotten more texts than the entire cheer squad sends in a week."

Officer Keller held out his hand. "May I see your phone?"

Automatically Mandy reached in her bag to find the pocket empty. "I left it at home. I was going to go get a new one tonight or see if I can get a new number."

"I'll give you an abbreviated police report, and your carrier should change the number for you for free."

That would help a little. "Thanks. There were a couple of scary posts on one of my feeds, but they disappeared while we were reading them."

"We?" The officer leaned forward.

"My roommate and I."

"What did the posts say?"

Mandy didn't want to repeat them. "Most of them called me names. Someone thought I needed an acid bath."

"Why didn't you report this to the police last night?"

Mandy blinked. "It never crossed my mind to call the police."

"But it did cross your mind to get a private security guard?" Officer Keller sat back and crossed his arms.

"Private security? No. We asked one of our artist friends and his husband to stay at the house last night, but Gordon is a sculptor."

He consulted his notes. "Then you didn't hire anyone from Hastings Security out of Chicago?"

"Officer, I am a school teacher. I don't have money for private security."

Officer Keller called into the hallway. "Mr. Alexander, would you come in here, please?"

The large man stepped into the office. He was built like one of the airbrushed muscle men on the front of romance novels.

"Mr. Alexander, you told me you were acting as a bodyguard for Miss Fowler. However, she seems to be ignorant of that fact, and from the way she is looking at you, I bet you have never been introduced." Though half a head shorter, Officer Keller didn't look the least bit intimidated.

"No, sir, we haven't. I was asked to watch out for her. And so I came to check on her classroom this morning."

"Who hired you?"

"I am contracted with C & O Enterprises."

Mandy sucked in a breath.

The officer continued. "Daniel Crawford owns that, doesn't he?"

"Yes, sir."

"Thank you very much, Mr. Alexander." Mandy couldn't help watching him leave the room.

The principal spoke up. "Your boyfriend must have hired him. That gets Mr. Alexander off my list."

"I don't have a boyfriend." She looked heavenward, hoping for a do-over, a candid camera, anything.

The policeman raised a brow. "Well, someone thinks you do."

Another policeman tapped on the door, a camera in his hand. "I'm all done in there. You can clean up."

Mr. Lee picked up the room phone. "Mrs. Janice, can you tell custodial they can clean A-103 now?" He listened for a minute before hanging up the phone with a thank-you. "Officer Keller, do you have any other questions for Miss Fowler? Students are starting to arrive."

"Just a few." The officer turned to Mandy. "I'd like you to look at your room and see if you can think of any art students who might be our perpetrators."

Mandy followed the men down the hall, noting Mr. Alexander's presence. Even knowing her room had been vandalized, she wasn't prepared for the mess. She slowly turned to take it all in—the broken window, the words painted on the easels and cupboards, her mess of a desk. The school computer had been smashed. Mandy was grateful she kept all her art files in the cloud. She studied the walls and the handwriting. "It is odd they didn't ruin any student art other than Roderigo's. And although they tried to copy his style, neither vandal is practiced enough."

"They?" The officer asked.

"Yes, there are two distinct handwriting styles going on. Notice the capital *B*'s and the *ch*. I think there may be a third as the blue paint on the front of my desk shows a lighter hand. She was also the one who painted the caricature on the board. Her strokes are not as bold as Roderigo's, but she did a decent job of matching his style. Too bad she isn't left-handed, I would have almost blamed him."

Principal Lee stepped forward. "You sure it isn't Roderigo? It looks enough like his work."

Mandy turned to face the principal. "No, it isn't his." She examined the board closer. "I'm positive it isn't."

"Then who?"

"Not sure." Mandy touched one of the letters. "They used tempera paint." She pointed to the white bottle on the floor—a brand made for kids. "It should wash off easily, but the red may stain. You may want to have the custodian check the manufacturer's website for tips on paint removal."

The officer examined some of the words. "Miss Fowler, any reason you say these were girls who wrote this?"

"The round lettering. In general, girls tend to write with a rounder hand." She turned to Mr. Lee. "Where should I teach?"

"Miss Fowler, I think you should take two or three sick days. With tomorrow being April Fool's Day, I'd rather you not be here."

"But I am not sick." Mandy crossed her arms.

The principal pondered her boot. "You have winced more than once since you walked into the school. I say you need three days of recovery time."

"But—"

"Look, Miss Fowler. With the threats you have received and the fact it looks like there was student involvement here, I think it's in everyone's best interest if you take some sick days. I have already approved the absence and called in a sub." The principal took a stance she had watched him use with belligerent students.

"Well, I guess I will sluff off, then." She turned to leave.

Officer Keller stopped her. "If you don't mind, we would like to look at your text messages. I can follow you home and pick up your phone. We will return it today."

Mandy bit her lip. There were some things on her phone that were personal. "I'll bring my phone to the station. I'd rather know what you are looking at."

"Fair enough."

Mandy eyed the truck in her rearview mirror. It had been following her since she left the police station. Two hours of her life she would rather forget. The truck was identical to the one Daniel drove, but the driver was not Daniel. When she pulled into the parking lot of the cell phone store, so did the truck.

Should she go back to the police station?

The driver exited the truck and came to stand by her door. Mr. Alexander. Mandy opened her door and glared. "You nearly had me driving back to the police station. Are you going to follow me everywhere?"

The big man crossed his arms. "Only until you get home and I can speak with you and your roommate. I meant to let you know before you left the station. I didn't intend to worry you. I'll wait out here." The man returned to the truck. Mandy was sure it was the one Daniel drove.

She was the only customer. Within minutes they assigned her a new number, and she left the store.

Mr. Alexander followed her home.

Mandy parked in the garage next to Candace's car. Shouldn't Candace be in class?

Mr. Alexander followed her into the house.

Mr. Alexander followed her into the kitchen.

At the table sat Candace with a man in his fifties who must be Mr. Alexander's workout partner.

The man stood and extended his hand, Mandy shook it out of politeness. Could this day get any weirder?

"I'm Jethro Hastings of Hastings Security. Have a seat, and I'll catch you up on what your roommate and I have been discussing."

Candace's mouth opened slightly as she ogled Mr. Alexander. "Mr. Hastings was going over the security measures he would like to add to the house and the alarm system."

"Alarm system? Seriously? No one needs an alarm system around here. Have you ever read the police report in the newspaper? They literally answer calls for barking dogs, and cats in trees. The most excitement they have had in months was the vandalism of my classroom." Mandy realized her voice was rising with each sentence.

"Miss Fowler, there have been credible threats made against you in the last twenty-four hours. Mr. Crawford feels an obligation to make sure you are safe."

Mandy mouthed "obligation."

"If you will please sit, I'll let him explain for himself."

Mandy took the seat next to Candace, and Mr. Hastings turned his laptop to face them. The C & O logo was replaced with a video feed of Daniel. Drat, he looked hot in a suit. It took Mandy a second to remember she was furious with him.

"My apologies in advance for cutting this short. They want me in the courtroom in ten minutes. Amanda, will you please hear me out?"

She would have to in front of his security men, so she nodded. Besides, she was powerless against those eyes. The screen must be HD.

"Yesterday when I called, I was trying to apologize for taking you out where people photographed us together, not for taking you out. It was irresponsible for me not to realize what might happen. I don't expect you to believe it, not with the new photos of Summerset trying to kiss me. Right now my main concern is keeping you safe."

Candace shrugged her confusion to Mandy's unasked question. New photos?

"First, let me have you meet Colin, my quasi-silent partner, friend, and 'techno geek' extraordinaire."

The video screen split, and they were joined by a man in glasses with messy hair. Candace grabbed Mandy's arm under the table. Definitely Candace's type.

"Hi, Mandy, Candace, nice to meet you. Although you are probably going to hate me in a moment." Colin's voice was seductively smooth, like a voice actor in an audio book, the hot-romance type.

Candace gripped Mandy's arm tighter. Hate was not on her mind.

"For the past thirteen days, I have had a bot monitoring Mandy's social media accounts. Yesterday when things started going crazy, I took the liberty of trying to further secure your email and blog."

"You have been spying on me? Isn't that illegal?" Only Candace's hand on her arm prevented Mandy from walking out.

Colin gave a tiny shrug. "On the social media, what you post basically has no privacy. The email puts my actions in a gray area but not outside the law so long as your provider knew I was there. But I would suggest you change your passwords on everything. Good job on suspending your accounts quickly yesterday."

Mandy wanted to scream, but she went into her calm-teacher mode instead. "Are you saying you read everything?"

Daniel jumped back in. "Amanda, a computer program scanned your incoming mail and posts for keywords, like the one your computer uses to determine if you have junk mail. Other than the flagged posts and emails, no human read anything."

"Flagged emails?"

"Yes, so far there have been about four, but only one of them was malicious. The bigger concern is the social media messages and the text messages the police pulled off your phone earlier today."

"Just a minute. How do you know about the text messages?" Mandy hadn't considered that taking her phone down meant she would end up reading more of the texts. In the end, she'd asked them to record what they needed and delete all the unread texts.

Daniel answered her question. "They gave Mr. Alexander a copy of them. As you said, this isn't exactly barking dogs, so Hastings Security offered its expertise."

The doorbell rang, Mr. Alexander went to answer it before either woman stood. Something offscreen took Daniel's attention away momentarily, but then he said, "I am sorry about this, Mandy and Candace. But please let them help you. Hopefully this will blow over in a few days and everyone will forget because there will be something more exciting in the news. I need to go. Mandy, please forgive me. May I have your new number?"

His feed cut off before Mandy answered, which may have been for the best, because the answer going through her mind was along the lines of "When my hamster learns to mop floors."

Colin was laughing. "Judging by your face, I'm assuming you will not be giving him your number today."

"Does it matter? I am sure you can find it, seeing how you managed to get into the rest of my life."

"I can, but I won't. You will need to give it to Mr. Hastings, but the choice to give it to Daniel is yours." The solemn expression Colin gave them made Mandy want to believe him. His gaze moved to over her shoulder. "Oh, wow. Where did those come from?"

Looking at the massive bouquet with a stuffed mallard attached, everyone in the room, including Colin, said "Daniel" all at once.

Candace jumped out of her chair and cleared a spot on the counter. "Oh, Mandy, he may have gone overboard, but these smell amazing." Candace buried her face in the blossoms. She plucked the card out of the pack and handed it to Mandy.

Colin was grinning. "Well, back to business. Hastings, did you draw up the security plan?"

"Yes. New locks, repair the fence, install an alarm system with some outside cameras, front and backdoors, and one in the garage. None in the house." Mandy was sure the security-team owner added that for her benefit. "We should be able to finish up by tonight if I can get my crew down here."

"On their way. Candace, Mandy, Mr. Anderson is going to take you to the county airport. You'll meet a plane with his team on it. The plane will bring you up to Chicago. Bonnie, Daniel's personal secretary, has arranged for you to have a spa day there while Hastings's men work on your house."

"No way." Mandy crossed her arms.

"Come on, girl. A spa day? In Chicago? That isn't going to be like getting a facial at the Cut n' Curl."

"Fine." Maybe there would be a hot masseur who would take her mind off everything.

"Ok, I'll see you two later." The screen returned to the C & O logo.

Mandy slowly got up from the table and retreated to the bathroom.

Studying her reflection in the mirror, she heard Grandma Mae's voice. *"Amanda Jane Fowler, what on earth have you done now?"*

The card she held in her hand had become little more than a crumpled mess. She smoothed the paper out.

Hank's grandson knows the truth. "Quack-qua, quack-qua-quack-quack."

Who knew ducks spoke Morse code? But what did he mean by N-Y? She had always been the one to say "not yet" when it was time to say good-bye.

She would give Daniel her number tomorrow—if she survived today.

nineteen

MANDY CHANGED THE CALENDAR. APRIL first. If anyone was a fool, it was her. Yesterday had been a nightmare and a dream all in one. Mud bath—they had actually taken a mud bath, and the massage had been to die for. Colin and Bonnie had met them for a private dinner. Colin had been adamant about them both changing their passwords for everything from Amazon to Zulily. Bonnie had not been what she'd expected at all. Daniel's secretary was grandmotherly yet feisty enough to make Mandy wonder if Daniel ran his office at all.

Mandy's toenails, painted with white flowers on dark peach, were mini works of art. In two weeks tops, they would be chipped and worn.

In two weeks her boot might be off. Hopefully. Had it only been two weeks since she'd fallen off the fence?

In two weeks she would be old news. Less if she was very lucky. Sunday's kiss attempt by Summerset Vandemark hadn't made the headlines. Fake, they had called it.

In two weeks her MFA project would be done. *If Only …*

In two weeks Daniel would be back. Or not.

People can survive without food for two weeks. She could do this.

She returned too late last night to call him and hadn't gotten up the courage to even text today. After seeing part of his life in Chicago last night, she wondered if she could ever live in his world. He'd be in court now so there was no point in texting yet.

At least the whole fiasco had given her two extra days on her project. She set about turning the Crawford mansion into an art museum with a statue garden and art classes on the lawn.

When a video-chat icon popped up on her computer, she clicked it open. Her parents never called in the morning. Mandy's mother's face filled the screen. Dirt smudged her cheek, and hair escaped the messy bun she always wore. "Oh, Mandy! Glad we caught you before work. My grad students showed me all the photos! How long have you been on crutches?"

"I told you about them last week, remember? Right before you told me about the stone pillar."

"Oh, that is right. Something about trespassing, right?"

Mandy loved her mother but had long ago realized that outside of the latest dig, she was incapable of focusing for long. It was ADD meets the Mummy's Curse. "Not exactly trespassing, but my foot is healing well."

"Who is this man in the photos? You didn't tell me you were dating someone." There was a distinct pout in her mother's voice.

"It is just Danny Crawford. Remember I met him the first summer I stayed at Grandma Mae's?"

"Oh. Why is your date all over the web?"

"He has low level celebrity status, that's all."

Mandy's father rested his head on her mother's shoulder. "I don't like some of the things people are saying about my little girl."

"I don't either, but the story will die down soon." Mandy didn't want to discuss the current status of her life. "How is the dig? Anything new?"

As expected, her mother launched into a detailed description of an intact tablet they believed to be of Chavín origin. Mandy only half listened. A tiny twinge of guilt nudged her for deliberately distracting her mother. But she was afraid if she mentioned the vandalism or her bodyguard, her father would abandon the dig for the first flight home.

In two weeks she would tell them the truth.

Two weeks was too long and not long enough.

Daniel studied the courtroom. The second day of testimony was well underway. A sketch artist in the corner scrutinized Daniel. At least there were no cameras inside. Dodging the ones outside had been difficult enough.

The EMT who had been punched by one of the photographers took the stand.

Across the aisle, Summerset sat with her father. Her soft-white suit and pink blouse reminded him of someone other than the party girl he knew. It wasn't until the single pair of pearl earrings caught the light that he realized she was trying to exude Princess Diana. If only she mimicked the late princess outside of the courtroom, he might have some peace. Of course, she was always better behaved in the presence of her father.

The bailiff called his name.

The assistant DA asked the standard identification questions before getting to the meat of Daniel's testimony. "Mr. Crawford, in your own words, please tell us what led to your 911 call the afternoon of December 29 and your subsequent actions."

"After lunch, I took a walk in Central Park to clear my head and make some calls. As I was returning to the hotel, I saw Miss Vandemark exiting. As always, there were a dozen or more photographers around. Miss Vandemark appeared to be more animated than usual. About the time I reached the corner, she collapsed. Someone yelled, 'She's not breathing!' and several of the photographers surged forward. The doorman tried to get them to move back. I dialed 911 and gave the pertinent info, then attempted to get through the crowd to her."

The lawyer reread his notes. "You are not a trained medic. Why did you try to reach her?"

"Miss Vandemark suffers from asthma and usually has an inhaler with her."

"Were you successful in reaching her side?"

"With the help of two of the photographers, I reached her about the time the police arrived."

"Which two photographers helped you?" The lawyer gestured to the courtroom.

Daniel pointed to Vic. "This one, Vic Jamison, whom I've met on occasion, and the taller man there with the gray sideburns, whose name I did not know at the time."

"Were you able to locate Miss Vandemark's inhaler and assist her?"

"Yes and no. The contents of her bag had spilled, and someone had stepped on the inhaler and broken it. I stood to tell the EMTs this and saw they couldn't get through."

"What happened then?" The lawyer took a step toward the jury.

"A whole lot of shouting, and me, Vic, the doorman, and the police trying to clear a path. Flashes going off, photographers still taking photos."

"Did you see who hit the EMT?"

"No, but I did see him go down."

"How long of a delay do you estimate was caused in Miss Vandemark's care?"

"Including my inability to get to her bag and an intact inhaler, at least ten, maybe twelve, minutes." As they'd agreed, he did not say anything about how the inhaler worked. There would be an expert witness for that later.

The attorney for the defense started his questioning.

"Mr. Crawford, did you at any time hit or push any of the photographers?"

"I pushed my way through the crowd and photographers, but I did not use excessive force."

"What was Miss Vandemark wearing?"

"Objection."

"Sustained."

"Other than locating the inhaler, did you administer any first aid to Miss Vandemark?"

"No."

"Why not?"

"One of the hotel employees was already administering first aid, and there was nothing I could do. As has been previously stated, I am not a medic."

"No further questions, Your Honor."

Daniel sat down, and Vic took the stand. At the break, the assistant DA informed Daniel he would be contacted if he were needed in the courtroom again, so he hurried to meet with the realtor about an apartment.

Daniel shuffled the papers in front of him and shifted his phone to his other ear. "Thanks for looking at the contract, Morgan. I don't want to be in the same hotel as Miss Vandemark, and I should be able to move in Thursday."

"You could move in tonight if you were willing to live without a bed."

"It's the desk I need. Between you, Colin, and Bonnie, I haven't had a chance to leave the hotel room since I got back last evening trying to keep up with work. I have one of those dates tonight, too, don't I?"

Morgan chuckled. "Not all the women we have arranged for your social calendar can fake eating bad sushi for lunch and cancel your evening plans just to get out of her contract like yesterday. At least tonight's is to benefit a school in Haiti and you both felt that was a good cause."

Daniel knew he wouldn't get another reprieve after both Monday and Tuesday night to himself. "You said you had news about the Indiana estate?"

"I had Colin put some documents on the secure server for you regarding the Indiana property. I'll never get the hang of all of that locking and unlocking. I didn't want to have one of the assistants do it. There must be some leak going on. I don't like the last offer one of the developers sent over—way too much money."

Daniel used the code Colin had set up last week to get into the secure folder. "There is some odd language in the original sale of the land to the Fowlers. It keeps referring to another agreement. Any idea what it's referencing?"

"No, but the mineral rights were retained by the Crawford estate. George Fowler sold his mineral rights to the property two years ago. The buyers must not have done their due diligence, or they would have realized the Fowlers never owned them. What is odder is that Mae Fowler deeded the home to a trust in Mandy Fowler's name when she was sixteen, but the property was sold out of the trust weeks before Mae died, using George's power of attorney."

"Have you found Mae's will?"

"Just the original with her husband, and he died twenty-five years ago."

"Something like that."

"I have researchers looking for the other document. Any chance your girl has anything?"

Daniel stiffened at the reference. "I am not sure if she does. She did mention she was to inherit the house. Not that it matters now. A tornado destroyed it."

"Ask her. I'll send you a copy of this latest offer."

"No rush. I don't think I want to take any offers dealing with gas drilling, not without protection for some of the land."

"I see."

"It has nothing to do with Amanda."

"I didn't say it did."

Daniel set the phone down. He had been getting offers for years now. But until this year, selling wasn't an option due to the one-hundred-year clause. As much as he hated the mansion, he loved the property. At least twice a year he went down to have a quiet few days, but there were other places to do that. He hadn't been as big a fool about the old mansion as Amanda believed he was. There were no leaks, and the broken windows had all been boarded up quickly. At least he hadn't sold the house to the buyers who'd wanted to turn it into a mortuary and private cemetery.

twenty

DANIEL HURRIED INTO THE COURTHOUSE. The verdict came in a day earlier than expected and would be read at the top of the hour, and the assistant DA felt all the key players should be there. His phone vibrated.

Colin: **READ THE NEWS**

Morgan: **Who leaked the mineral report?**

Bonnie: **Don't you dare** …

He raised his brow at the last one, turned off his phone, and tucked it into his briefcase before going through security. He would have to wait until after the verdict to figure out what was going on.

The jury only deliberated forty minutes. It was, after all, one of those slam-dunk cases every DA wanted. Even without the testimonies, there were hundreds of subpoenaed photos from that evening, including several of the EMT's bloodied nose. As expected, the judge made an example of the three photographers who had chosen to plead not guilty and pay the initial fine.

One would think the paparazzi would be on their best behavior for a while, unless they happened to be exiting the courthouse. There had been fewer photographers at the last television awards banquet. Daniel turned back into the courthouse to wait them out. Unfortunately, his 180 brought him right into the arms of Summerset, who was standing on the step above him. Her mouth landed on his and her arms wrapped around him. Conscious of the narrow stairs behind him, Daniel didn't jerk back as he removed her arms from around his neck and stepped to the side.

Summerset gave him a pouty look. "Why, that was the worst kiss I have ever received."

"That would be because I didn't kiss you."

The unanticipated slap landed hard enough to cause him to step back and nearly lose his balance.

Once he'd steadied himself, he turned, plowed through the paparazzi, and hailed a cab.

On his way to the apartment, he turned on his phone and opened the link Colin had sent him. *A refinery?* Never. He nodded at the doorman while still trying to read the last of the article. In the privacy of the elevator, he let out an audible groan. It wasn't often he reached the point where he wanted to hit something. Best hide away for the rest of the day. Fortunately his social calendar showed a Thursday-night hiatus. He hoped the furniture had arrived so he could sit down and work.

It had.

He picked up an orange-and-purple pillow and threw it at the yellow couch. For good measure, he punched the pink chair with stainless steel trim and stomped on the flowered carpet.

No one had warned him the decorator was colorblind.

Thursday found Mandy at her usual 4:00 p.m. appointment with Dr. Christensen.

He frowned at the images on his tablet. "I must say I am disappointed with this last set. A museum and a country club are solid, but they don't stretch the imagination, do they? Not like today's news about the refinery."

"Refinery?"

Dr. Christensen reached into his blue recycle bin and pulled out the front section of the *South Bend Tribune*.

Mandy read the headline twice. "May I keep this?"

"It is a gimme, but I think you should do one with what the property would be like with a petrochemical refinery on the site."

Mandy half paid attention. How could Daniel do that to Hank's great-grandson? He had promised. She should have called last night or the night before. But she didn't know what to say. Thank him for the bodyguard or say good-bye? If she spoke to him now, she knew she would yell. What would Grandma Mae tell her to do?

Mandy had no idea.

She dialed his number, but it went straight to voicemail.

Mandy entered from the garage. Candace and her law-school friend were sitting at the table in a heated discussion.

"Is it true?" Candace held up an *IndyStar* with the same headline as the South Bend paper.

Mandy pulled her own out. "It's in multiple reputable papers, it must be. I don't think the big syndicates retract many stories. I tried to call Daniel, but it went to voicemail. I am having problems believing he would sell the land for a refinery." She hadn't left a message. He might see the new missed call with her area code.

Candace tapped her legal pad. "We are planning a rally for Saturday."

"It will hit the news cycle better if we hold it Monday, providing anyone pays attention to my emails." The law student looked as though he had been arguing for a while.

"Are you in?" asked Candace.

Mandy sorted through the mail sitting on the counter. Two envelopes from the hospital. Probably her ER bill. She opened one as she answered Candace. "With Mr. Alexander on my tail, it doesn't matter. He wouldn't let me anywhere near a rally. Do you know how hard it is to teach with an observer in the room and half your students lusting after him?"

"Oh, let me guess. They wanted to use him for the live model—shirtless." Candace giggled.

Mandy rolled her eyes. "Thankfully, my classes are not up to life drawing. Although one of the girls did manage to work him into a reflection of her still life. He kept my third hour petrified and Coach Robb from coming on to me in the teacher's lounge." Mandy sighed. The coach would not lay a hand on her for quite a while. The handshake Mr. Alexander had given him had stopped short of breaking bones. She had no idea what the conversation had been, but she hoped whatever was said kept him away for the rest of the school year.

"What did Coach Handsy try this time?"

"I was getting the mail out of my cubby, and he came up behind me. Mr. Alexander was so fast it barely registered that Coach was saying something about a 'tight end' and trying for one of his hands-on approaches." Mandy paused and reread the check. "That is odd. The hospital sent me a reimbursement."

The law student focused on her through his thick glasses. "Have you ever filed a harassment complaint?"

"Half the single women in the school have, but the team is winning, so we get to put up with it." Mandy rolled her eyes before trying to read the letter from the billing department. "Have either of you ever heard of the insurance covering your deductible, too? This letter says my March ER visit has been paid in full. That doesn't make any sense."

Candace took the letter. "It wasn't paid by your insurance. See the code on the copy of the bill? It is a different acronym. Looks like a third party."

Mandy took the letter back and stuffed the paper back in the envelope. "There must be some mistake."

"Back to our protest." Candace pulled out the paper she had been doodling on. "Are you in?"

Hank's grandson swam across her mind. "If it is true, maybe. But I think the story needs to be verified." Mandy focused on Candace, not wanting to break the unwritten rule of talking about other guys in front of potential boyfriend material. "I think that techy friend you have may have the connections to verify this. You should contact him."

Candace jotted a note on her pad.

"As for me, I had my next picture for my MFA drop in my lap. I hadn't thought of destroying the mansion." She plucked a wilting rose from the bouquet and vowed to try to call Daniel again.

"Oh, did you read the paragraph where DC turned down an offer to make it a mortuary and private cemetery?"

"Missed that, but I did that to the old church." Mandy hurried to her room.

twenty-one

CANDACE WATCHED OVER MANDY'S SHOULDER. "You sure you can't toss some smoke or smog into that?"

"I already explained that this type of refinery runs clean. There won't be any smoke." It had taken more time than she intended to get the refinery to completion. Part of her problem was a lack of stock photography, so she'd made most of the pipes from scratch. Consistent lighting still plagued her.

"It sure is hideous."

Mandy grinned. "Anyone who sees this photo would think so. I added a few extra pipes. If you look carefully, the pipes spell out *ugly*. I wanted to try that whole '70s subliminal thing."

"That's it." Candace bounced up and down, causing her periwinkle curls to dance. "We can use this for a poster!"

"I'm not sure about that." Mandy bit her lip. "I think that would move it to the published category, and all my works are to be unpublished so they can go up for sale to benefit the college."

"Can you come up with another idea? Or another version of the refinery?"

"I'm running out of time and ideas. I still can't believe Daniel would sell the mansion for this." *Even if he does hate it.*

"Have you talked to him? Colin must have sent ten texts asking you to. He is having a tough time not giving Daniel your number."

Mandy didn't mention the three calls that had gone to voicemail. The one voice message she started to leave was only half his name. "You saw those photos yesterday of him kissing Miss Moneybags after the verdict. He doesn't need the girl next door." *I need to stay out of his life.*

Candace huffed. "Remember? Not everything in the tabloids is true. If it were, Daniel would be out there with an $80k camera shooting it up with the best of them."

"Let it go. On the bright side, I am pretty much yesterday's news. Colin said there hasn't been a threat to me in over twenty-four hours."

"When did you talk to Colin? I have tried to reach him all evening to verify the story."

Mandy double-checked the clock on her computer screen. "He texted before lunch. By the way, I told Colin to give Daniel my number. If Daniel is desperate to talk to me, he has a strange way of not calling."

Candace tipped her head. "It has only been a few hours. Maybe he is busy."

"Busy dating every socialite in Manhattan. Wednesday night was a date for a benefit, and he has probably left for tonight's outing with the rich and spoiled."

"Are you following those fangirl sites?"

"Not today." Mandy hung her head. "He kisses them, too."

"Let me see." Candace scooted Mandy out of the way and pulled up the browser. "That is a side-hug cheek kiss. It doesn't count at all!"

"If your lawyer friend gave you one of those, you would count it."

"That is only because I don't think he has ever even kissed before. He can barely touch my hand without blushing. And he has yet to ask about my hair. I went through three different wigs yesterday."

Mandy laughed. "Totally normal to have your girlfriend go to the bathroom and come back with a new do. Is he your date tonight?"

"No, I told you Friday night is girls' night. Just us and a few of our friends. Pizza, ice cream, and every Meg Ryan movie ever made."

"Mr. Alexander isn't going to like that. Too many people in the house and pizza delivery coming."

Candace winked. "Not one bit."

Daniel cringed as he opened the door. The designer had removed the hideous pink, orange, purple, and yellow furniture, including the flowery rug, and gone masculine. More like a hunting lodge. The taxidermy bear standing in the corner would give someone nightmares. Him.

He texted the designer. **Do you have any rental furniture that is more neutral and somewhat comfortable?**

I'll see.

— At this point Ikea would be an improvement.

Oh, I can do that only better.

He checked the calendar on his phone. April Fools' Day had ended four days ago. Why did he feel he was stuck in it?

— I realize it's Saturday. But I would like something more relaxing for the weekend.

No problem, Mr. C. I'll be over in an hour.

— I'll have the doorman let you in.

Meeting the person who kept turning his apartment into a circus was not a good idea. He needed a shower and to get out of here before his next date. He was going to fire Morgan and the legal team. Being seen with six different girls in one weekend was not easy. And not as fun as it should be. But then, they were all playing a part as per their contracts.

Leopard skin. She had replaced his bedspread with a leopard skin.

He wished he had a New York version of Terrance who would call up Bloomingdale's and order him a set of six hundred-count Egyptian cotton sheets, a nice navy comforter, and a recliner. That was all he needed. That and towels that were not zebra striped. How was a man supposed to dry himself off with zebra towels?

While he waited for the car service to arrive, a text came from Colin—the first in several days. Colin didn't enjoy it when his partnership duties forced him to travel, even for computer-related business.

Meeting with the Tokyo group going well. Meant to text this earlier. M. 574-555-1607. Don't blow it.

The car arrived with Dublin LeDuc ensconced inside. Daniel smelled her overpowering perfume before he saw her. He'd have to wait to call Amanda. He hoped the new superhero movie was good. It had better be to make up for dealing with red-carpet paparazzi. For the life of him, he couldn't remember what role Dublin had played. He should have reviewed his memos.

The clock changed from 11:59 p.m. to 12:00 a.m. Monday.

She glanced at the silent phone. Not even a text. She'd left a short voicemail asking him to call, rerecording it twice. He'd gone out with six different women this weekend and not five seconds to text her. Perhaps she should have done a Summerset and slapped him after the kiss at the pond. Maybe her heart would hurt less.

At the time, she'd thought the kiss last Saturday had meant something. He'd claimed he wasn't a player. But she had checked this week's date photos using an analysis program. Those photos were not manipulated. More than half of the women had kissed him in public. She didn't even want to think about what might be happening in private. What kind of fences did they have?

She analyzed the quote in the laundry room another way. "Good fences make good neighbors but lousy lovers. No matter how she twisted it, the fence between them was more than chain link. If it was the old pole fence, at least they could climb through it.

Never would she trust her heart again. Danny had grown up to be a spoiled, conceited, lying, handsome (no, scratch that)... She tried to come up with another adjective, but only things like *funny*, *caring*, and *tender* came to mind.

She was yesterday's news. No, yesterday's news was Daniel's countless dates, ending with some awards thing for some type of music, a perky blonde on his arm, her lips mashing his, her jewel-encrusted dress worth more than a camera.

Six hours ago, Mr. Alexander had told her he would not be shadowing her anymore and had given her a panic button, telling her to use it even if only for the coach. Then he shook her hand and left.

She was not going to cry. Anymore.

She would not dream of DC.

And the reason she wasn't sleeping? Her foot hurt. It had nothing to do with the kiss that kept replaying in her mind as often as those she'd seen on the entertainment channels. Why was she defending him?

The last thing she thought of as she wiped her nonexistent tears on her pillow was that Candace's rally started at three. School got out at 3:20. Hank's great-grandchildren would not lose their home if she could help it. She owed Daniel nothing.

twenty-two

DANIEL WOKE FEELING DISORIENTED. WERE the steps going up or down? What kind of designer put an M. C. Escher knockoff on a bedroom wall? The same designer who had done his entire apartment over in black and white with construction-worker orange accents. The couch was at least comfortable, even if it did resemble a huge, smashed toilet-paper roll. And the desk was pure Ikea, plain and functional. He could live with it for another week. At least he didn't have to go to court today. There had been a jury issue over the weekend, and they'd needed to choose new jurors. His phone rang. Odd. Mr. Hastings almost never called.

He tried not to sound too blurry. "Crawford here."

"Sorry to bother you, but we have a problem at the Indiana property."

Fully alert now, Daniel sat up. "Is Amanda okay?"

"At the moment, yes, but her chameleon-haired roommate and lawyer boyfriend have set up a rally at the mansion this afternoon."

"Protesting what?"

"The sale of the property for a refinery."

Daniel collected his clothes from the closet. "There isn't going to be a sale. We put out a press release."

"Well, they missed the local paper. We started finding flyers for the rally late last evening."

Daniel ran his hands through his hair and pulled his phone away from his ear to check the time. 7:43. "Let me think. Colin is en route from Japan, so he can't help. If I can get a ticket, I should be there around two or three." He'd talk with Candace, then he could spend an hour with Amanda.

"We could talk to them, or you could call..."

"No, the trial was postponed until tomorrow. And I want to see for myself how Amanda is doing."

"I suggest you charter a plane. Then you won't have the drive from the airport to deal with."

"Probably right. I'll let you know the details when I do."

Daniel stared at his phone and wished for a split second he had a New York office, but Father hated the Big Apple. Getting the apartment must have made him roll over in his grave. Daniel laughed. Perhaps the designer was karma.

Too early in Chicago to call Bonnie, Daniel found a charter company they'd used before and hoped the last-minute flight didn't cost him as much as he thought it would. What time did Amanda need to go to work? After he met with Candace, should he call her or go see her?

Mandy had forgotten she had an art-department meeting. She pulled up the lane just after four to find about fifty people there, mostly college students. But she recognized a few of the older locals, too. Candace was shouting something unintelligible through a bullhorn.

She pulled the poster board sign out the back of the Golf Ball. Keeping the sign low, she moved toward the crowd. Candace wore a cheap red-white-and-blue wig, the type a clown would wear on the Fourth of July. She started them chanting.

"No gas here! No gas here!"

She came over to Mandy. "What do you think?"

"I think that is the worst wig you have ever worn and I made a mistake coming here. Look, Candace, it's only us and some cows across the street. Did you ever talk to Colin?"

Candace blanched. Apparently not.

Just then, three vehicles came speeding down the road. Two had satellite equipment and network logos on the side. The third was an all-too-familiar truck. No. Mandy couldn't see the inside clearly, but the driver who passed the access road to the main gate wasn't built like Mr. Alexander or his crew. Mandy felt her heart sink a little lower. She moved away from the crowd. One of the news vans had boxed in her Golf. Mandy turned around—better to hide in the middle of the crowd. Maybe the cameras would miss her.

The camera crews unloaded their equipment out of the van, a reporter questioned various protesters. Someone pointed toward Candace. Mandy moved to the other side of the crowd, closer to the fence, wishing it offered more protection.

Dust rose from the road near the house.

The truck.

She froze for a moment, then turned her back to the fence and hunched down behind the picketers, hoping not to be seen.

Candace's voice rose above the crowd. "Anyone see Mandy?" Several people answered. Candace found her and tugged on her sleeve. "They have got to see your sign."

"No. You show it. Do you see who drove up?"

Candace looked over her shoulder. "Why, it's the man himself."

"I've got to get out of here. Where is your car? I can't do another week like the last one and being on TV with him."

"I came with—Oh no. Too late. He's taken an interest in your car, and now he is scanning the crowd. He isn't smiling."

Mandy wished the boot off. The only way she could get lower was by sitting. "Get away from me so he won't notice!" She pushed her roommate and the sign away.

A reporter, microphone in hand, came to stand beside Candace. "Miss, I understand you're the organizer of this rally?" Candace moved several yards farther away and grinned into the camera.

The blonde reporter flashed a smile and asked her first question. "Why do you feel saving this old house is important?"

"This house is a work of art. It deserves to be more than a photograph in an archive or a crumbled-down ruin. I was inspired by a project my roommate is creating called 'If Only…'" Candace lifted Mandy's poster and showed the picture of the beautifully restored mansion. "See, like this, repaired and beautified, the estate could become a great asset to our community." Candace flipped the sign over. "But this is what a refinery would be like here."

Mandy wasted no time working her way to the far side of the crowd, keeping low. There were some trees on this side of the fence if she could get to them.

The reporter studied the picture. "Where did you get this photo?"

"My roommate created it."

Mandy dropped as close to the ground as her boot and skirt would allow.

"Is your roommate here?" The reporter scanned the crowd.

Don't look at me, don't look at me, don't look—

Several people in the crowd pointed Mandy's direction and moved away.

"Young lady?"

Mandy looked up from her crouched position. When the reporter addressed her, Mandy mouthed a silent "me?"

"Yes, you. Are you her roommate?"

Mandy stood up and dusted off her skirt. The camera was aimed at her face. "Found my keys." She held her key ring up. Lame.

Candace tried to step between the eager reporter and Mandy. "Yes. It's her MFA project. Let me tell you—" But the reporter stepped around Candace.

"Impressive work, miss." The reporter turned to the cameraman. "Get a shot of the sign." She turned back to Mandy. "Why do you want to save this house?"

"I…um…I lived near here when I was a child. And I hate to see another piece of our history morph into a parking lot or concrete structure. There are few buildings left of this style."

The reporter tapped the piece in her ear. I have just learned Mr. Crawford is here and will speak to us." She turned her attention to Daniel crossing toward them through the crowd. Someone spit on him. The saliva dripped down his shirt, but he walked with purpose, giving heed to none of the jeers and insults flying around him.

The reporter shoved the microphone in his face. "Mr. Crawford, what do you have to say about this protest?" A reporter from the other network joined her.

Daniel focused on Mandy as he answered. "I think the protesters need to do their research and not rely on erroneous newspaper articles."

"Are you saying you have no intention of selling this land?"

"The statement C & O put out Friday afternoon clearly stated I have no intention of selling this property to see it marred by a refinery. C & O is no longer conducting any business with the company credited with starting the rumor."

The color drained from the reporter's face. She'd obviously neglected her research too. "Are you looking to sell your ancestral home?"

"I have been entertaining several proposals for the future of this property, but no final decision has been made. And anyone who thinks I would sell this to make a refinery doesn't know me very well. I already gave my word that parts of the estate would remain intact." He dipped his head slightly in Mandy's direction.

The reporter whirled back to Mandy. "Aren't you that plain Jane who enjoyed a romantic meal with Mr. Crawford last week?"

Mandy felt the heat rise in her face. Most of the protesters stood stock-still, their signs lowered. Backed nearly to the fence, Mandy had no place to run, even if she didn't have the boot on.

Candace tried to step between Mandy and the reporter. "It appears we were mistaken. Our deepest apologies to Mr. Crawford. Come on, people, move out!"

The other reporter cornered Daniel. "Mr. Crawford, do you have anything more to say?"

Mandy felt his eyes on her, but she didn't look up.

"I don't have anything to say that anyone would listen to." He turned and walked off.

The tenacious reporter came back to Mandy's side. "Mandy, can you answer the question every woman has been asking all week? How did you end up on a date with Daniel Crawford?"

"It wasn't a date. It was a good-bye." Mandy ducked her head and hurried after the crowd.

twenty-three

DANIEL SLIPPED BACK THROUGH THE gate and into his truck. If only he had called Mandy this weekend or even texted her, he could have prevented this entire thing. He had planned to be here hours ago, but a fuel-line problem had forced him to wait for another plane. Not being able to reach Colin, he couldn't get Candace's number, and Amanda had been working, so he hadn't even tried.

He knew she'd called over the weekend, but the façade he'd worn for the dates would have cracked if he spoke to her as he wouldn't have been able to go on the next outing or the one after that, and the "overload the paparazzi" thing was a necessary step in countering Summerset's advances for his upcoming testimony. But from the look on Amanda's pale face, he knew the act had cost him what might have been real.

From the cab of the truck, he saw her sitting in the still penned-in car. He dialed her number.

Amanda answered on the second ring. "I'm sorry. I should have stopped it." Her voice wobbled—whether from poor reception or tears, he wasn't sure.

"No, I should have returned your calls. I just—I should have called." The sound of the news van starting up echoed through the line.

"Thanks for the bodyguard and paying my hospital bill."

"Not a problem. I caused both messes." He watched her little car spring to life.

"Good-bye, Danny."

His phone beeped to indicate the call had ended. He watched until the Golf drove out of sight.

Mr. Alexander met him before he got to the door of the caretaker's house. "You don't want to go in there. Channel 5 is replaying the feed now. I know I am speaking out of turn here, but I have followed her all week now. I have seen her put up with a bunch of crap she didn't ask for. Not once has she fallen apart. She spent most of Saturday and Sunday checking her phone for a call she never got. I've had several assignments as your bodyguard, sir, and I will tell you this. She is better than ten of those society girls you paraded about with all weekend. Those were real tears in her eyes, not some crocodile job the cameraman caught as she unlocked her car."

"I'd appreciate it if you would take me to the airport."

Mr. Alexander mumbled something.

"If you called me an idiot, you have things about right. And you aren't fired." Daniel leaned back in his seat and rubbed the bridge of his nose.

Candace didn't bother knocking. She just walked in and sat on Mandy's bed. "I am sorry, Mandy. I finally found the press release buried in the financial section of Sunday's paper. He did issue a statement."

"It isn't all your fault. I could have tried harder to check too... Each new photo of someone clinging to him...I let my personal feelings cloud my judgment." Mandy turned to hug her roommate.

Candace pulled back from the embrace. "You need to come to the living room. Mr. Alexander is here, and they are putting through a video call."

"I don't want to see him."

"Mr. Alexander?"

"Daniel."

"Okay. Let's go talk to Mr. Alexander."

Poor Mr. Alexander. Candace's furniture was not built for his overly large frame. "Miss Fowler, I know you may not want to hear it, but I am back on bodyguard duty until Colin and Bonnie determine I am off."

"Did he ask you to?"

"Yes. While we hope the news story doesn't generate new threats, Mr. Crawford agrees it is better to be proactive this time."

"Do you have to go to school with me?"

Mr. Alexander nodded. "I know my presence is distracting in the classroom. How about I check your room in the morning and hang out in the teachers' lounge? You have your alarm, and I can be there in seconds."

Mandy gave a half smile. "I may call you in for my third-hour class. They behaved better on Thursday and Friday than they have all semester."

"Sure, I can come in if you need me. And I will be there whenever that coach might be around."

Candace looked up from her phone. "Video feed will be on in a minute. Don't worry. Colin says it is only him."

The computer screen flared to life, and Colin's face filled the screen. His eyes drooped, and his speech was slower than normal. "I owe you two an apology. I was in Japan working on something and got back a few hours ago. I took a prototype phone, and it didn't handle all my text messages well. Had I known what you were planning..." Colin gave a shrug. "I am not exactly asking your permission this time, but I am monitoring all online activity regarding both of you. Candace, so far I've found three email accounts for you plus a catchall. Do you have any others I should know about?" A list of her emails appeared on the screen.

"You are missing the one for my children's-hospital support activities for kids dealing with cancer. It routes through the hospital." She typed it in.

Colin rapidly typed on his keyboard. "Hmm, this one will get me into HIPAA-compliance issues as well as dealing with minors. And there are some lines I won't cross. How about you tell me the second anything odd comes through."

"Sure."

"Okay, sorry again for this. But with the trial, I think the media will mostly ignore the protest. As for the fangirls, they are too busy trying to figure out Daniel's dating tour of New York, so with any luck, nothing will happen this time." The screen went blank.

Mr. Alexander stood. "Ladies, let me check the cameras, and then I'll leave you to yourselves."

Mandy turned to Candace. "Do you know what stinks? Now I need two new pieces for my show. With the ones on the poster all over TV, I can't say they are still unpublished."

Daniel checked his phone as the plane bounced through the landing and began to taxi. It would be nearly ten by the time he got back to the apartment. Not for the first time that day, he was glad he had no social engagements for the evening. Daniel's stomach growled. He hadn't taken a moment to stop and eat something substantial all day. He might have been better off if he had chosen one of the more expensive options for the charter that included food. But his father had instilled a few too many of his miserly ways in Daniel. He really should have found a commercial flight to save him money considering how, in the end, he saved no time. And to think he had been trying to save on the apartment.

Once they were on their way to the apartment, he sat back in the limo he'd booked with the charter. What would the driver say if he asked him to drive through the Golden Arches? Daniel decided to order takeout and have it delivered to the lobby. He made a quick call to the doorman and placed his order online.

His phone beeped. Colin.

You know you are an idiot for not contacting her earlier, right? Nothing like having a best friend who was blunt.

— Pretty much. I wish I could explain the dates.

You will be glad to know there have been no threats this time.

Daniel sighed in relief. Usually the threats came immediately. Four quiet hours had passed. Hopefully nothing would happen.

— Do you think she is out of danger?

Not sure. Keeping Hastings on it. BTW, Bonnie is TICKED.

— I can only imagine.

I doubt it. I am rather annoyed with you too.

Colin and everyone else he knew.

— Join the club.

Aren't you going to fight for her?

— How?

Figure that one out yourself.

Daniel leaned his head back. He didn't have a single clue. He dialed Mandy's new number. Voicemail. He tried again. On the third time, he left a message. "There is probably nothing I can say that will make you call me back or listen. Please, not good-bye, not yet."

The takeout bags were still warm. He gave the doorman an extra tip.

Daniel stepped into the apartment, then stepped back out to check the number on the door. Somehow the decorator had gotten things right. Warm colors, comfortable looking chairs, and clean lines.

At least one thing had gone right today.

twenty-four

"BUT, MR. CRAWFORD, I HAVE a few more touches to add to your apartment." No mistaking the New Jersey accent of the high-pitched voice.

Those touches worried Daniel. "Please, you have done enough. I'm quite happy with the interior as it is. Will you please send me your final invoice?"

"Are you quite sure? The bedroom could use some more color."

"Positive. It is perfect."

Another call beeped through. Morgan. "Thank you. I do need to go." He switched over to the new call.

"Daniel, why did you fly out to Indiana yesterday? Couldn't you have called?" The exasperation in his lawyer's voice filled the room.

"I thought I would get there before the protest started. I didn't think a news van would come to blink-and-you-miss-it Indiana to record fifty people protesting. They had no way of knowing I was there before I announced myself." He knew that wasn't the truth. He'd wanted to see Amanda and thought he would have the opportunity after shutting down Candace's rally before it started.

"Well, one thing good came of this. That mock-up your girl did of the refinery has gotten attention. People don't want it. And as far as other news, the clerk over in the courthouse in the county to the north managed to dig up the missing document. Apparently there is an agreement going back to your great-grandfather at the end of the Great War. The bottom line is that the Fowler property can be passed from generation to generation of Fowlers but not sold to anyone but the Crawford heir, and the sections of land not used must remain in their natural state. In the sixties, there was some question about the deed, a second sale of the land occurred for one dollar to register the deed properly. How the documents ended up in the wrong courthouse is anyone's guess."

"So George Fowler had no right to sell it?"

"Correct. The other thing is, we are relatively confident the signatures that allowed the property to leave the trust were forged. But we need to talk to Miss Fowler to be certain."

The new couch was as comfortable as the toilet-paper one. "What does this mean for the Fowler property now?"

"Well, we can contest the sale, and I think we will win. I have no idea what the current owner will do, but they will probably go back to Fowler and demand their money back. But we need to have Mandy listed as one of the plaintiffs since the last legal transaction was to the trust in her name."

"You know she isn't talking to me?"

Morgan's dry laugh came over the phone. "I heard. Good luck."

According to his watch, he needed to leave for court for the opening statements in half an hour. So far the media had not picked up on the fact he was testifying on behalf of the hotel, not the Vandemarks. The gossip rags had been too busy following his social life to focus on the reason he was in the Big Apple in the first place. The next three days should be interesting.

While he waited for the car service, he opened the scan of the original Fowler sales contract and began to read.

Another phone message from Daniel. At least he had come up with a new angle, but using Grandma Mae was low. Mandy deleted the message like she had two others since last night. He should know the meaning of good-bye.

It was best if they stayed out of each other's lives. Of course, it was difficult to forget him when Mr. Alexander stood in the doorway of her classroom, arms folded over his chest. Mandy waited for him to say something or leave.

"You really can go. My room looks fine."

Mr. Alexander gave a mock salute. "I'll be around."

Mandy wondered if he had a first name, but it wouldn't matter. Hopefully by tomorrow he would be gone.

Nothing out of the ordinary happened during her first three classes. During her prep hour, she completed the cleaned-up version of the mansion from a different angle, adding different landscaping and painting the wood trim a warm gray. She glanced at her clock. If she hurried, she had time to collect her mail before lunch. She still had the untouched blueberry bagel from breakfast in her desk. The room tilted as she stood. Skipping breakfast had been a bad idea.

Drat! Coach Robb was the only person in the room. At least she only needed to get her mail. Reaching into her cubby, she suddenly felt his breath on her neck. "So, I see you are in the market for a real man. Mr. Money Bags doesn't seem to want you."

Mandy cringed. Should she hit her panic button? She turned, keeping her handful of papers up as a shield. "Back off."

"Darlin', don't go all frigid on me." He put his giant hand on her shoulder, pulling her shirt forward in the process, his eyes dropping to her chest.

"Please move." She pulled the papers back to cover her gaping blouse and tried to step to the side.

His hand moved to the side of her neck. "Baby, I—owwww!"

Suddenly he disappeared.

No, he was bent over a table, one arm twisted around his back.

Where Mandy expected to see Mr. Alexander, a tall, athletic brunette stood. "Perhaps my boss wasn't very clear last week. Leave Miss Fowler alone." The woman stepped back.

The coach's face burned red—from anger or embarrassment, Mandy couldn't tell. He took a menacing step toward the new woman. "Well, well. What do we have here? A woman with beauty and brawn. Perhaps you—"

"Would like to file a sexual harassment complaint?" she said to Mandy.

Coach took another step and raised his hand to the newcomer's shoulder. In a flash, he was face down on the table again.

"Or I can give some self-defense lessons to the teachers at this school. You are easier to take down than you look."

The door opened, and three teachers walked in, their laughter fading as they took in the spectacle. The shortest female started laughing again. "I've wanted to do that to him forever!"

The science teacher adjusted his tie. "Do you need any help?"

"Would you kindly go get your school officer? I believe your coach needs to be arrested on assault charges."

The coach let out a string of profanities.

When the resource officer and the principal appeared, the brunette stepped back, keeping the coach restrained.

"Just what is going on here?" Mr. Lee walked to the coach's side.

The coach opened his mouth, but the woman spoke first. "I witnessed this man sexually assaulting Miss Fowler. I would like you to arrest him."

The principal stepped away from the coach. "Arrest?"

"Yes, I believe in this state, the charge is sexual battery." The brunette looked to the short teacher. "Possibly multiple counts."

"Miss Fowler, do you agree?" The officer pulled out his cuffs.

"She doesn't have to. I witnessed it, I can bring the charges."

"And who exactly are you?" asked the principal.

"Abbie Hastings, of Hastings Security."

Mandy felt like she might faint.

And she did.

Two trips to the ER in the space of a month. At this rate she should get a frequent-patient pass. The doctor had recognized her, but the boot may have helped.

"There you go," he said as he set the half-empty glue tube on the tray. "Unlike stitches, with glue, there should be no visible scarring on your cheek. Let's peek at those X-rays. Good. No fracture to the cheekbone, and your foot is healing nicely. Another two weeks and you can take that boot off."

Not exactly good. A week longer than she planned. She would still be wearing the boot for her MFA show.

"I'll have someone come in with your paperwork, and you can leave."

Mandy sat up and faced Abbie. "Thanks for your help. Did you really have him arrested, or did I imagine everything?"

"*We* did. Between what Alex witnessed last week and what I did today, there is a case there. The short teacher also filed charges. I won't be surprised if other women step up to add more counts."

Wincing, Mandy stopped mid-nod. "Yes, I know at least ten who have filed harassment complaints with the district."

"Alex guessed as much."

"Alex?"

"My brother. He goes by Mr. Alexander on the job. I'm part of his team. You didn't think he was the only one watching out for you?"

"I hadn't thought about it."

A woman in scrubs entered with a clipboard full of papers.

Mandy signed the necessary forms and followed Abbie out.

"Oh, just so you know, I'll be living with you and your roommate until the Vandemark trial is over."

The automatic doors opened with a whoosh. "Why?"

Abbie pointed the way to her car. "Mr. Morgan, Daniel's lawyer, is worried about repercussions. The Vandemarks don't like to be crossed. And Daniel's testimony could go either way."

"But how does that involve me?"

"Because hurting you hurts Daniel." Abbie opened her car door.

"But we are not dating or anything. I am just an old friend."

"Keep telling yourself that and maybe someone will believe it. I've spent the last three years around Mr. Crawford, and, believe me, he doesn't want you hurt."

If he didn't want me hurt, then he should have never kissed me. Mandy looked at her foot. "Really?"

"Yup. Oh, I need to take your photo."

"Why?"

"Miss Fowler, if you need an explanation, a thirty-year-old single female bodyguard is the wrong one to ask." Abbie Hastings snapped the photo. "It is for Daniel. He needs proof."

The doctor had to be wrong. She must have a concussion and was hallucinating the conversation.

Daniel hadn't been called to testify today, so he couldn't break his date tonight. His being in the public eye kept Summerset from blogging that they were having private trysts—an added benefit to the defense team's strategy. He hoped they were correct in their assumptions of the Vandemark legal team's plan, or else all these dates were for nothing. Considering the number of times Summerset had tried to ambush him the last ten days, being seen with many different women was a good idea, even if he was beginning to detest every minute of it. He scrolled through his calendar to figure out the who, what, and when of his evening. It could be worse. At least he wanted to see the Broadway revival of the show. If he ate enough garlic for dinner, the smell might keep his date at bay. Doubtful. After her seminude performance at the music awards last year, she had been sleeping her way through the A-list. It would take a silver stake to keep her limited to the one-kiss clause of the contract.

In the cab, he checked his phone. The second he got into the elevator he called Mandy. Voicemail. "How are you? What did the doctor say? Please, please call me, Amanda." If only the trial were over and he could explain all the dates and public kisses. He begged Morgan for an exception to explain to Mandy, but the lawyer was too concerned too many people knew the truth about the dates, and he was nervous, even with the nondisclosures that had been signed.

His next call was to Hastings. No answer.

His third was to Bonnie. Voicemail. "Please, I need help. This can't get any more messed up!"

It could, and most likely would. His date was in an hour and a half.

She'd licked him.
Cameras flashed.
The world shuddered.

twenty-five

"I WANT TO KILL YOU or fire you. I can't decide which." Probably not the best way to start a conversation with one's lawyer. Morgan only laughed and said he had felt the same way about Daniel over the years.

"Please, Morgan, give me one piece of good news. Other than it's Wednesday afternoon and the week is half over."

"How about your date's people called to tell your people that she is sick of people?"

"Really?"

"Yes, go to the Rangers game alone or skip it. After all, you have work to do. And I hate to tell you this, but it looks like you need to go to London again for some PR shots with the new buildings and a ribbon cutting."

"No." *I need to go to Indiana. I need to fix things.* Daniel looked at his calendar. "That is Mandy's MFA show." The words came out in a whisper.

"What did you say?"

"Nothing. Go ahead and book it. I need to go. Lunch break is almost over."

"I hope they call you to the stand today."

"Me too. I think the Vandemarks have realized I am here for the defense even though their lawyers subpoenaed me too. Summerset looks like she can't decide if she wants to kill me or seduce me."

"Watch your back."

Four hours later, on the bottom step of the courthouse, Daniel wished he had taken his mentor's advice literally. The screech of "Da-a-an-i-i-e-l-l-l!" matched a computerized falling-bomb effect, with the explosion landing on his back.

Summerset wrapped her arms and legs around him and rained sharp little kisses on the back of his neck.

And the cameras flashed.

Then she slid off his back and stood on the step behind him but kept her hands on his chest. "Darling, you must stop playing hard to get."

Daniel spun around and stepped back disentangling himself. She moved in for a kiss, but Daniel threw his hands up to block her. "Miss Vandemark, you forget yourself. I have other plans this evening." He slipped past a cameraman and hailed a cab.

Mandy texted a response to Daniel's voicemail to acknowledge she was okay. To do less would be rude, especially when he'd picked up the hospital bill again. She'd sent four texts since yesterday afternoon. All of them impersonal and short. She needed their relationship to be a thing of scrapbooks past.

His mansion loomed large on her screen. Her additional meeting with Dr. Christensen had not gone well. The dean had not been pleased that her designs had been on television but had been mollified when her manipulations had been praised by extension from the university's Art and Design school. She needed one more variation of the mansion by Monday for the show deadline. Fortunately, this would be a touch-screen piece, so she didn't need to take the time to print it onto canvas or render it on a 3-D printer.

Unfortunately, the touch screen would allow people to zoom into nearly pixel level, so her work had to be flawless. Dr. Christensen wanted her to email him a tight comp by 9:00 a.m. Friday. That left her a little over thirty-six hours, and seven of them she needed to be at school teaching.

School turned into another disaster. Memories of the football players' glares at her and the female teachers' smiles made it difficult to focus on her work this evening. She didn't send Rodrigo to the office for his cartoons about the coach's arrest. But she had kept them. It wasn't her fault he was arrested, as the administration had fielded complaints for years.

Abbie and her brother traded off following her. Apparently Daniel still hadn't testified. The Vandemarks had brought in several experts, and the news channels were calling the trial the most snooze-worthy of the century. Good. Daniel needed some boredom in his life after all those dates.

Not having a single idea for the photo, Mandy went in search of sustenance and found Candace and Abbie eating popcorn and watching Candace's favorite cable channel.

The eight o'clock show started—a celebrity gossip affair. Daniel Crawford was the lead story. The three women sat glued to the screen, mouths agape at Summerset's back hug. Photos of all his dates over the past week flashed across the screen—the kisses, the hugs, and the lick.

There were no tears to prick Mandy's eyes. Instead, her stomach rolled, threating to send back up the popcorn.

She ran to the bathroom as fast as one could run in a medical boot and rinsed out her mouth. A wicked thought entered her head. Dr. Christensen would disapprove, but she couldn't resist. The idea was original, and it would push her skills to the limit, requiring hundreds of manipulations. Did such a place even exist outside of the Old West? Possibly in Nevada. Mandy hurried to her room and turned on the screen. She had research to do.

Tacky hot-pink buildings, garish signs, and suggestive names filled one screen. Mandy flipped through the mansion photos, wishing she had one taken from a drone. But then, with the crutches, she had only been able to take the photos from a few angles. Still, better than the fence shot.

Oh! That gave her another idea, and her favorite stock photo site obliged.

Early the next morning, Candace tapped on her door and entered. "Didn't you sleep? I came to see—Oh no! You can't!"

Mandy didn't look up from her work. "Why not? I think it is a perfect use of the building for him and all his friends. Even men like Coach Robb would find the place enjoyable."

"But it is a brothel!"

"*Bordello*, aka brothel with some class."

"I know you are mad at him, but this is going too far. And the hot-pink shutters are too tacky to be called classy. The swimming pool looks like a—No, Mandy! I can't believe you would do this."

"Look closer." Mandy zoomed in on some of the windows. One had vinyl lettering: "No tops allowed, bottoms optional (but frowned upon)." Several other windows boasted activities worthy of bodice-ripper romance covers.

"You can't do this. Isn't it slander?"

Mandy shook her head. "Every photo I used is from a stock-photo site, and although some of the men may be blue-eyed, tall, and sandy-haired, none of them are DC."

"Where on earth did you find statues and topiary so ... so ... risqué?" Candace pointed to a garden and maze and a large gazebo with a bed at the center. "They are like triple-X versions of Rodan's Kiss."

"They are highly manipulated stock photos from a pretty trashy site."

"Trashy or pornographic?"

"Technically art nudes, but I have seen some rather shocking things." Mandy gave the tiniest of shudders.

Candace sat down on the bed. "Mandy, I am sure this is good therapy, but you realize this image can never leave this room. He only took you to dinner and kissed you once."

"Yes, and thanks to that, I have had death threats and my schoolroom vandalized. I've been humiliated on TV—okay, that was our fault. And the same lips that kissed mine—did you see those photos last night?" Mandy burst into tears, all the pain of the last two weeks trying to leave her body at once.

Candace wrapped her arms around Mandy and let her cry. There wasn't enough fudge extreme ice cream in the world to solve this one.

twenty-six

DR. CHRISTENSEN'S VOICE WAS TIGHT on the other end of the phone. "Yes, I have seen more risqué pieces from my students, but are you sure you want to do this?"

Mandy squashed the twinge of doubt like she would a spider daring to invade her bathroom. "I only have a few working hours. This is the best I have short of a tornado piece, and you know I can't do one of those after the one hit three years ago. And I already did a car burial ground, and I think a cemetery is too cliché."

"Very well, change the shape of the swimming pool and soften some of your statues. The work needs to be appropriate for under eighteen, and those aren't exactly Michelangelo."

Abbie came into the room, and Mandy quickly hid her work.

"Thanks, Dr. C. I'll send the finished one over on Monday morning."

Abbie stepped around easels. "Alex got word Daniel is testifying after lunch. If all goes well, you'll be rid of me in a few more days."

Too bad. Other than not being artistic, Abbie was a great room-mate.

The moment the defense had waited for had come. Daniel Crawford took the witness stand.

The attorney got right to the heart of his questions. "Last week in another trial you testified you tried to help Miss Vandemark by using her inhaler. Why did you think her inhaler would help?"

"Over the past couple of years, Miss Vandemark has had three such fainting spells in my presence, all of them brought on by a combination of stress and alcohol." Daniel looked at Summerset's father, hoping he would understand the danger his daughter had become.

"Had she been drinking?"

"She had one glass of wine at lunch, although I cautioned her not to."

"Any particular reason for that, Mr. Crawford?" The attorney leaned in.

"Yes, Summerset rarely is able to stop at one drink, and I knew lunch would be distressing for her."

"What reason did you have to believe she would be distressed?"

Daniel shifted his eyes to meet Summerset's. She needed to listen this time. "Because I told her I was no longer interested in pursuing a relationship with her, and I felt she needed to enter a sobriety clinic as I could no longer be that for her, since keeping her sober had somehow become my job."

The judge hit his gavel three times to quiet the court.

"And what was her reaction?"

"She threw her lunch at me."

"And what did you do?"

"I signed the bill and left the restaurant."

"Did you see Miss Vandemark again that afternoon?"

"Possibly. A half hour later, I left the hotel to take a walk. I thought I saw her through the doors to the bar, but the glass is wavy, and I didn't check to see if my assumption was correct. I had previously asked the bartender not to serve her and assumed that if it were her, she would be turned away."

"Were you aware the bartender you had spoken with had left for a family emergency around one and had been replaced by another?"

"Not until the testimonies were given on Wednesday."

The attorney checked a paper on his desk, then addressed the judge. "That will be all."

The prosecuting attorney rose for the cross-examination. "You say you broke off your relationship with Miss Vandemark that day, but were you not, in fact, leading her on?"

"No, sir."

The lawyer held up three photos. "In the last two weeks, you have been seen and photographed either kissing or holding Miss Vandemark."

"As the tabloids will attest, I have been seen with several women over the last several months and weeks. All of them were dates or outings at my invitation. And several of those women have also kissed me. All the times I was with Miss Vandemark, the kissing was at her instigation, with the exception of the Academy Awards, where we had both been invited as guests of one of the nominees for best actor."

The voices in the room rose. The judge banged his gavel again.

"So, you are some type of womanizer?"

The defense attorney stood. "Objection."

"Sustained. Do you have anything relevant to ask the witness?" The judge glared.

The prosecuting attorney checked with his partner. "No, Your Honor."

Daniel stepped down from the stand.

Summerset jumped from her seat. "You! Liar! You said you loved me! You told me you would help me!"

Mr. Vandemark tried to pull his daughter back into her seat.

Daniel continued to walk out of the courtroom to the banging of the gavel and the screams of Miss Vandemark.

Until the trial officially ended, Daniel was stuck in the city, but at least he didn't have to endure any more dates with the too-willing women of society. And maybe, just maybe, Mr. Vandemark would do what he should have done months ago and check his daughter into rehab. Closing arguments would be Monday, the verdict no later than Tuesday. He had a Tuesday-night flight to London. He sat down at his computer in the apartment.

Mandy still answered his calls with texts. **I meant it when I said good-bye**.

He'd sent flowers.

She texted a photo of them donated to a retirement home.

Now that he could finally explain the dates, she wouldn't listen. Had the ruse been worth it? Yes, the strategy had shut down any claim Summerset had made about their relationship, left the hotel blameless, and hopefully got Summerset the help she needed. But Mandy also believed he was a player of the worst kind.

The only good news of the day had come from Morgan via email. There wouldn't be a trial over the Fowler property. George Fowler had confessed to forging Mae's and Mandy's signatures. Mandy's father surfaced from a dig long enough to be outraged and confirm he had no interest in the property. And the holding company that had bought the land turned it over to Daniel's possession without a fight. The transaction had been accomplished quietly, without Mandy needing to be involved. He hoped George Fowler possessed half a brain and had invested his $3.4 million wisely.

He needed some other way to convince Mandy to give him a chance. What had the love therapist been talking about on the radio when the driver had picked him up the other night? Or was it that television noise he had on? What had they called it? The final move? No, the "grand gesture."

Daniel logged into the password-protected file and opened the deeds and purchase agreements, then he brought up the land map and called Morgan.

Then he texted Colin.

Who needed flowers?

If this idea worked, Mandy would talk to him and, more importantly, listen as well.

The image blurred in front of Mandy's eyes. She bit her lip and finished her diet cola. Doubts filled her. She had toned down several of the manipulations, and none of the men in the windows resembled Daniel. If she had three more days, she would abandon this manipulation entirely, but in five hours, school would start and the image needed to be in. She cleaned the vinyl sign from the window and replaced it with a simple "shirts and shoes optional." The pool was transformed into a heart surrounded with heart-shaped hot tubs. Chubby cherubs, leaves, and scarves hid things some considered art when sculpted by Italian Renaissance artists.

It would raise eyebrows, and the student newspaper might even comment, saying she hadn't pushed boundaries enough, but technically the work was solid. She ran it through several web programs that detected image manipulation and managed to fool all but one. It didn't like the wooden fence she'd designed, but she was too tired to figure out why.

She uploaded the photo to Dr. Christensen's cloud, then set her alarm, half hoping it wouldn't actually go off.

Everyone crowded in the courtroom to hear the verdict. Outside, photographers vied for the best spots.

The attorney for the Vandemarks asked to approach the bench. Summerset's usual place next to her father was vacant.

The verdict was never read.

Mr. Vandemark apologized to the hotel.

The rumors flew. Summerset entered a rehab clinic in Idaho. Unrest in the Middle East topped the news stories.

Daniel boarded a plane bound for London and sent a group text to Colin, Morgan, and Bonnie.

I don't care how much it costs me. Figure it out. Only funds from my personal accounts. And under no circumstances use a decorator from New York.

He turned off his phone.

twenty-seven

THE LONG EMERALD EVENING GOWN Mandy wore to the Champagne reception for the opening of her show Friday night had once belonged to Grandma Mae, back in a time when a woman would never have been seen buying groceries without her face done. Candace had put Mandy's hair up in a French twist and even decorated the boot in case it peeked out under her hem.

Mandy walked through the exhibit answering questions. The son of the gas station owner beamed as he pointed out details.

A minister from the denomination who owned the rundown church asked her questions about restoration costs that Mandy couldn't answer. He didn't seem to understand that she wasn't an architect or contractor.

Mr. Alexander stood next to Bonnie and pretended to be interested in an old house from the 1920s as he kept watch over the room. Mandy avoided talking to them. She didn't want to talk about Grandma Mae's house. It was what had started the project. The opening photo was the one she'd taken the morning after the tornado, when part of the chimney still stood, along with some of the lath-and-plaster walls.

Dr. Christensen introduced her to an executive from a software company, the tech guru complimenting her work. Then the dean came and whisked the executive away to see the old grain mill.

Candace's natural-looking wig matched Abbie's dark hair. The two chatted over hors d'oeuvres with Colin near the train-station shot.

A distinguished-looking gentleman who'd come in with Bonnie was examining the Crawford mansion and chatting amiably with her father. Her mother monopolized Principal Lee.

Mandy was still in some shock over her parents coming and declaring they would stay in the States through graduation, in late May. They hadn't mentioned those plans during their weekly phone calls or emails and had planned the surprise for months and even left a dig for her—for an entire month. Of course they would be working on papers and research, but they were here.

Daniel sent a corsage. She'd worn it because it went with the dress. At least that was what she told Candace. The note indicated he was in London and asked her to make it "not yet" instead of good-bye.

A reporter asked her a few questions. None were about Daniel.

Later that night, as she hung up the dress and turned out the lights, Mandy would wonder how she remembered so little of a night she had worked so hard for.

And the smell of Daniel's corsage would fill the room like a fairy tale. If only...

As Mandy walked around the room, taking one last look, the dean hurried in. "Miss Fowler, I am glad I caught you. We had a whole-show bid! That hasn't happened for eight, no, nine years!"

"But the gas station man wanted some of those pieces."

"Yes, I told the bidder that. He said he would sell a duplicate at a reduced price."

Mandy stopped in front of her favorite piece. "What about the two I wasn't going to sell?"

"That is the problem. This is an all-or-nothing deal. You can keep the files for personal use and for your portfolio, but you can never exhibit them."

"There is one I don't want ever displayed. I want to destroy it."

The dean rung his hands. "Miss Fowler, perhaps you don't understand the magnitude of this sale and what it will do for the college."

"How much is Daniel Crawford paying you?"

"He isn't the buyer. The buyer is British. Has the most calming accent I have ever heard."

Mandy paused in front of a monitor. "Can I stipulate the bordello version of the Crawford mansion never be shown in public?"

"I don't know. Come to the office. You can ask. I think it is midnight there, but he insisted I call back."

The dean was correct. The man's voice was calming. Mandy had already forgotten his name—Clarence? Or maybe Terrance? Whomever he was, he responded to her request with "Why do you not want that piece exhibited? It is an excellent piece of manipulation."

"It was a mistake, sir."

The line crackled. "I saw no errors in it."

"No, an ethical mistake. It would have been better to turn the building into a haunted house." Mandy didn't want to explain further to some guy, no matter how soothing his accent.

Even the robust-sounding laughter that came over the line sounded British. "No house is better off haunted if one can avoid it. We have our share of ghosts over here."

Mandy tried a different tactic. "Well, the fence is wrong in it. It still shows as fake in the detection programs."

"Not an issue. You can tear the fence down or repair it on your copy. But if you insist, it will never be shown to the public. Only in private viewings."

The dean studied her anxiously. Mandy knew how desperately the money was needed. "Thank you, sir. I will sign the papers."

"Thank you, Miss Fowler. I am sure you have an exciting career in front of you." His accent made the prediction believable.

When the dial tone filled her ears, she set the phone down and signed the forms.

On the way home, she picked up a burger and fries. As she walked into her kitchen, she realized she had forgotten her shake but then remembered the last time she'd had a shake and fries. She tossed the bag in the trash. Food was overrated.

For days Daniel had nightmares that the New York City decorator had gotten access to his other residences. Terrance and Bonnie laughed when he told them. But he didn't believe he was safe until he stepped off the elevator into his Chicago penthouse Sunday afternoon.

Mr. Vandemark had sent him a note thanking him for trying to help Summerset. There would be no retaliation. Time to pull Hastings's team off Amanda. He put in the call.

For a while he waded through emails and the reports he had set aside knowing if there were a real problem, some VP would have contacted him directly. Colin had the correct idea—focus on the parts of the work you love. The only reason Colin hadn't made that stupid top one hundred list is few people knew Colin Ogilvie as the current *O* in C & O. Yes, he showed up at annual board meetings and kept up with the major dealings, but he spent most of his days surrounded by his computers, contributing to the tech end of the business by inventing new things. Daniel had been somewhat surprised he had left his little tech cave to see Mandy's MFA show, even if he did want to try out his new button cam.

Daniel brought up the footage and watched it again. Colin had streamed the entire thing live. He had been gratified to see Mandy had worn the flowers he had sent, but her smile was tight and her laughter guarded. As suspected, Colin focused on Candace when he wasn't showing the exhibit. He hadn't noticed the first time he watched it, but the frequency with which Candace's name entered the conversation made him look twice. During the live feed, Daniel had focused on Mandy, trying to assess the toll the last month had taken on her, hoping to catch her voice and wishing she would smile. He flipped off the computer. Even though he'd only recorded Mandy in a public place, he still felt somewhat dirty, like an old peeping Tom.

He turned the computer back on and deleted the files.

twenty-eight

DANIEL SAVED THE ATTACHED PHOTO to the cloud before reading the email again.

Daniel,

Thank you so much for sending the corsage. It matched my dress perfectly.

I'll be honest. I'm glad you couldn't come to the show. The local paper was there, and it was a relief to not be asked about you. You live in a world that resembles a fish bowl. I am a Swainson's Warbler (one of the shyest birds in North America, in case you are wondering). You need an angel fish or even a dolphin to share your life with you.

I can't live a life with bodyguards—though thank you for sending them—or where if I run to the store without makeup people think they can photograph me.

I suppose that some birds and fish can be friends, depending on size. Can we just go back to being friends who shared a summer? Maybe one day your fishbowl will shrink.

You will probably be tempted to call. Please don't.

I really do need this to be a good-bye. We can be the type of friends who like posts and send Christmas emails. Someday we will run into each other at a Cubs game or something and exchange a hug.

I wish you the best.

_ _ · _ · · ·

Mandy

PS. When I see you at the game, I owe you an apology. But it is too hard to explain. It's another reason I am glad you didn't come.

The bordello. Poor Mandy. She must have been hearing Grandma Mae's voice scolding her over it ten times a day. Too bad. It made him smile. She had done a magnificent job with it. He looked at the attached photo again and wondered where she had found the vintage gown. He saved it to her profile in his phone, then started to look up the Cubs schedule but remembered she wasn't a fan. Fighting for her had just moved to a whole new level. How much could he ditch the paparazzi and his fans in the next few weeks? Shouldn't be too hard considering how much work had managed to wait for him and with his empty social calendar.

Pondering the plans he'd set in motion, it hit him. It had been in an interview with a couple on their seventieth wedding anniversary. The reporter had asked them if they had any secrets to their successful relationship. The husband stated that he made it a point to kiss her good morning and good night. His wife had blushed when she admitted that he still brought her a single flower every Friday. The therapist had it wrong. Love wasn't in the grand gestures; they weren't real. One of the reasons he wanted a relationship with Mandy was that she was real.

Mandy's mother turned as far as she could in the pedicure chair. "I haven't done this for years. How different is this from that spa in Chicago you went to a couple of weeks ago?"

More like a month and a half ago, which was why she agreed to a new pedicure for graduation, but she had already explained that to her time challenged mother. "No comparison, starting with the robes they had us change into." Mandy leaned back as the manicurist pulled her foot out of the water.

"I can't believe how much not being on a dig for three weeks has let my nails grow. We haven't had a chance to spend much time together since you started college. I miss this."

"Me too."

"When are you going to stop moping around?"

The exfoliation tickled, and Mandy shifted before answering. "I'm not moping."

Her mother raised her brows. "And I have a hamster that types."

"Is that how you get your papers published so quickly?"

"Amanda Jane, I am serious. I know you told that Danny boy good-bye, but are you sure you did the right thing?"

Mandy looked around the room before answering, wondering who might be eavesdropping. Only the manicurists were in earshot. "Mom, the fact I am checking to see who is listening should be answer enough. I just can't do that my whole life."

"But if you could find a way, wouldn't it be worth it?"

"Mom, please."

"I haven't seen him in the gossip columns since that silly trial ended."

"Have you been looking?"

Her mother reached over and patted Mandy's arm. "Hasn't every woman under fifty-five?"

Most of the employees, including Bonnie, had left for the night. Daniel pulled out his phone. **Can friends text?**
Sometimes.
— What do you call a duck that steals?
No clue
— A robber ducky. Later. Daniel set his phone down.
Another text came. **Bye.**
At least it wasn't *good*-bye. Daniel considered that a small win.

The restaurant was crowded with mostly graduates and their families. Mandy debated telling her parents about the scones. "I am glad you are here for my graduation."

"Did you really think I would miss my little girl receiving her master's? I would fly halfway around the world for it. Oh. I did!" Mandy's father laughed at his own joke.

"Gerald," her mother chided before turning to Mandy. "Have you been here before? What would you recommend?"

"The salmon is excellent."

Her father set down his menu. "Dr. Christensen told me the scones were the best. I think I will order some for desert."

Mandy didn't dare eat one.

— What do you call a bird that can fix anything?
IDK
— Duck Tape.

172

Thanks for the graduation flowers. They are lovely.
— Later

— Two ducks are in a pond. One went "Quack, quack!" and the other duck said, "That's funny. I was just about to say that!"

— What do you call a duck on drugs?
Stupid?
— A quackhead
These are bad. You quack me up.
— Later
Kk

Daniel stared at the responses. He squelched the desire to high-five Terrance as he sat in the backseat and watched the eye of London turn in the distance. A month of texting had earned him an agreement to his 'later.'

"What has caught your fancy, sir?"

"Nothing."

"Nice to see you smile again. Now, here is the agenda for the next meeting."

Trying to focus on the information, Daniel's mind went back to wondering if they could move beyond jokes. He was running out.

twenty-nine

"HEY, MANDY! ARE YOU UP there again?" The wrought-iron steps clanged as Candace climbed into the loft.

Mandy looked up from *Wuthering Heights*. Reading the novel was the only way the novel would ever get off the shelf. She had once chosen it as her "do not disturb" book but had vowed never to kiss a guy again, or at least not for the rest of the year.

"Not that book again." Candace flopped down and took the book from Mandy. "Your Friday flower arrived—a perfect red rose."

Mandy didn't touch the flower Candice held. Was it the sixth or seventh. She had lost track. "Did I tell you he texts me every night? Duck jokes."

Candace didn't answer. "Let's go to a movie or something. You have hidden up here for weeks. Didn't you finish *Tristan & Isolde* yesterday? Enough with the tragic love stories. We need to celebrate. School's Out for Summer!" The last few words were off key, if it was possible to be off key when singing an Alice Cooper lyric.

"It's Friday night. Don't you have a date?"

"Not very observant, are you? Larry the Lawyer tossed me like a hot potato after the protest. I didn't have a single date in May."

Mandy sat up. "How did I miss that?"

"That I didn't have a date or that the calendar turned to June?

There wasn't much to miss. If he hadn't ended it, I would have. He always talked about himself. Can you believe he never once asked me about my hair?"

"No. Isn't he like the third person to not ask?"

"Other than employers, pretty much. What are those papers?"

Mandy handed her the stack of printed emails and a couple of snails that came to the university. "Mostly job offers."

"The CIA? Seriously?" Candace held up a letter on cotton paper to check the watermark.

"Apparently they have graphic-design jobs too."

Candace finished flipping through the papers. "California, New York, and London? Are you considering any of these?"

"Who wouldn't consider London? I got my new school-district contract, and even with the increase in pay, any of these offers is double or more. Well, maybe not the CIA. I am sure they can't tell me my pay unless I accept, not that I am seriously considering them. I can only imagine the type of work I would be doing for them. Part of the reason I did the master's was to get a pay raise."

"Do you still like teaching?"

"I don't know. So many of my students don't want to be there. And since the coach has been fired, there are several kids who resent me. Did I tell you they caught the vandals? The head cheerleader was the ring leader. Her parents are blaming me. I haven't figured that one out yet. The sad thing is, she has some real art skills."

"Am I losing a roommate?"

Mandy shrugged. "There are a couple jobs I can work from here."

"Oh, then we can be the old art ladies. I have a new commission piece. If I get enough of them, I can stay in my studio all day. We'd get a couple of cats." Candace tossed a throw pillow at Mandy, who snatched it out of the air.

"You are allergic, aren't you? Besides they would probably take over the lover's loft, and then we would have no place to hide."

Mandy set the pillow down and slid off the beanbag.

"Lover's Loft? Considering no guy has been up here for ages, I think the room needs a new name. Come on. Let's go to dinner at the Chinese place and catch a movie. There is a new one tonight with that hot actor."

"Which hot actor?"

"Does it matter?" Candace laughed as she led the way to the garage.

Colin opened the door to Daniel's office. "Still working? You should take a break."

"This coming from the man who regularly puts in eighty hours behind his computer? There must be an ulterior motive."

"You know me too well, my friend. You need to go down to the mansion and see what the crews have been doing."

"I've been getting reports."

"To which you have been giving one- and two-word answers. I'll drive."

"Do you even know how?"

"I have a license. I just never use it. I think I have a red car I have only driven once or twice."

Daniel shook his head. "That is a Lamborghini, and if you want to keep a low profile, which I do, it's the wrong car. We can take my car."

"Good. I left my duffel on Bonnie's desk. I don't like driving that far."

The caretaker's house was empty, as Hastings's security team had left, choosing to hire a local firm to watch over the property since they were more bodyguards than guard dogs. Daniel made the necessary call to let the local firm know they were on the property.

Colin pulled open the refrigerator door. "Tabasco and an expired yogurt." The freezer held a bag of peas that testified they had been used more than once as an ice pack. "Even the cupboards are bare. Let's go get something. I am starving."

Daniel tossed Colin his keys. "You go."

Colin raised his eyebrow. "You sure you want me to drive?"

"No one can know I am here."

Colin disappeared through the door. An engine came to life, followed by a sickening thunk-thud. Daniel winced. By the time he reached the car, Colin had already inspected the damage. "I only damaged the trunk—car and tree."

Daniel rolled his eyes at the bad pun. "Promise me never to ever back up in your Lamborghini."

"But it is in my garage. I'd have to back up to get it out." Colin held up his hands in surrender.

"Precisely. Hop in. Let's go get some food."

"Just admit it. That was a terrible ending. I swear the actress cringed every time she kissed him."

"I agree. Zero chemistry. How can you not have chemistry with him?" Mandy smiled.

"You know by now that chemistry takes more than good looks. Remember when we both thought Coach Robb was hot?" Candace opened her car door.

"Then he opened his mouth." Both girls laughed.

"Ice cream?"

Mandy groaned. "I feel like that is all I have eaten this month."

"Okay, then we can get some sorbet, too." Candace headed her car in the direction of the little local market.

Only one checkout was open, and the cashier sat pondering her nails. Candace made a beeline for the frozen foods with Mandy in her wake.

"Raspberry-lemonade sherbet. That looks good." Candace licked her lips.

Mandy grabbed a couple of frozen dinners before joining Candace. "It would be a change from 'Chocolaty, Choc, Choc, Chocolate.'"

"Hey, Candace," a voice called from the end of the aisle, "nice hair."

Mandy froze. Colin? Here? And Daniel?

Candace tossed her pale-mint ombre locks. "This old thing? How kind of you."

For a moment Mandy considered diving under the cart or crawling behind the half gallons of vanilla. Too late.

"Candace. Mandy." Daniel nodded at them.

"Isn't this a coincidence? We were getting ice cream. Any chance you two want to help us eat it?" Candace grabbed a half gallon of fudge ripple and added it to the cart.

"Sure, I'm game." Colin added a container of vanilla.

To Mandy's mind, Colin seemed too eager and Candace too bouncy. Coincidence? More like elaborate setup. Mandy took a step back.

Daniel stepped forward. "You got your boot off. How does your foot feel?"

Mandy looked at her matching flats peeking out from under her maxi skirt. "My foot feels fine, but it's funny to walk normally again." Mandy backed into the cooler shelf.

"Careful. You don't need an accident tonight." Daniel lifted his hand and brushed her cheekbone with his finger. "It looks like that has healed nicely too."

Mandy told herself it was an odd scar thing sending tingles dancing across her face. "You know about—? Never mind. Of course you do."

"I tried to call you that night. You didn't answer."

"Hey, you two, the ice cream is melting. We will check out, and I'll take Colin back to our place. Daniel, can you drive Mandy?"

"May I?" Daniel dropped his hand and stepped back.

Mandy didn't trust her voice, so she nodded. Daniel raised his hand and waved. "It looks like I still need milk." He moved back up the aisle to where Colin had abandoned their cart. By the time they reached the checkout counter, Candace and Colin were gone.

Mandy followed Daniel to his car.

He pointed out the huge curve in the back end. "I'm not sure the trunk will open, let's put these in the backseat."

"What happened?" Mandy traced the dent with her finger.

"Colin. He has never been an attentive driver, but now I am wondering if it was deliberate."

"Why would he crash your car?" Mandy slid the last bag into the backseat.

Daniel deposited the empty cart in the cart return. "I wasn't coming to the store with him."

"You think they set us up?"

Daniel opened her door. "Of course I do, and if you finally talk to me, his ploy will be worth the repair bill."

Mandy watched him round the car and get in. "I'll talk. You have been rather persistent in the weeks since my MFA show. But when we are done and I say good-bye, will you let it mean adieu?"

"If that is what you want, I will. Do you mind if we drop off my milk before going to your place for the ice cream?"

Mandy turned in her seat to face him. "Sure. And I need to say I'm sorry."

"For what?" He turned north towards the estate, a road Mandy had avoided since the protest.

"I did a final manipulation of your mansion I shouldn't have. I was angry, and I thought you—never mind. It doesn't matter what I thought. It was beneath me, and unkind."

"The bordello? That one is hilarious. You probably designed the pink monstrosity when I was in New York, and with all of the dates I had, you probably thought I deserved it."

Mandy stared out her window, not sure how to respond.

"I need to explain about the New York dates. They were all setups. Mutually beneficial appearances complete with contracts and nondisclosures. My goal at the trial was to get Summerset into rehab, but I needed to get her father to hear me this time. As long as she maneuvered the press to tell her version of reality, her father would believe her. I spent the past three months in an ever-escalating frenzy of dating that peaked during the trials keeping me in the public eye, building evidence that Summerset and I were not exclusive. The photos made it difficult for her to claim a private liaison. All my contracted dates knew we were acting, and, no, they weren't paid. They only got the publicity. But then I went on one very real date. And they wouldn't let me tell you about the others. My guess is you did a less-tame version earlier. After the lick kiss and Summerset's last stunt, I think half of the web gossips would have turned my house into worse if they had your skills."

Mandy's head whipped up. "Did Candace tell you about the first one? How much have you been spying on me?"

Daniel reached for her hand. "Other than the reports from Hastings, which did not include photos other than the one of your cut cheek, which you knew Abbie took, I only spied on you once for about two hours."

"When?" Mandy narrowed her eyes.

"The opening night of your show. Colin was wearing a button cam. I wanted to be there and to see everything, but I was stuck in London working on the opening of the new restaurants. I wanted to ask your permission and have you wear the camera, but—"

"I wasn't returning your calls".

Daniel turned onto a narrow paved lane.

The road was unfamiliar to her. "Where are we?"

"Back gate." He touched a button on his dash, and the gate swung open. He drove through and parked behind the guesthouse. "I'll take these in and be right back."

He had wanted to be at her MFA. And he'd basically contracted all the dates, including the kisses. She processed the information. Hired dates did make them even closer to the brothel scenario.

No wonder he'd laughed. Mandy studied the two-story house. It made sense he would have been staying here. The building couldn't be seen from the road. Even when she had lived with Grandma Mae, this part of the property hadn't been visible. But the old caretaker had let them play on the rope swing and with his cats. And his wife made snickerdoodle cookies better than Grandma Mae's. This house would have been a happier place. The kitchen light darkened, and Daniel returned and slid into the driver's seat.

Mandy placed a hand on his arm. "You don't need to apologize for the button cam. I doubt you saw anything you wouldn't have had you been there. It wasn't like Colin followed me into the restroom."

Daniel cupped Mandy's face. "Do you know what I did see?"

Mandy swallowed but didn't move. His hand felt so right it made her wish for a lasting relationship.

"I saw how sad you were. How when you smiled, you didn't light up. How you avoided the brothel—"

"Bordello sounds classier."

"Bordello and Grandma Mae's house. I wanted to crawl through the computer and hug you. Tell you I was sorry and explain about the dates. I was ready to hop on a plane and come back and skip the ribbon cutting. Terrance talked me out of it."

Mandy tipped her head. "Terrance? How odd. That is the name of the Englishman who bought the entire show, including Grandma Mae's and the bordello. I didn't want to sell them."

"I know." Daniel let his hand drop.

Mandy's hands flew to her face. "He works for you, doesn't he?" Daniel owned them. He had been able to study the bordello in detail.

"Yes, and, as promised, they are in my private collection. So, I am curious, have you managed to get the fence the way you like it?"

"I haven't worked on it."

"And another question—why are you standing in the attic in the old yellow dress?"

Mandy turned to face the window. "I am sure I don't know what you are talking about."

"Still a terrible liar. Do you want to know what I think it is? I think you hoped I would come find you because I am not really a player."

Mandy gasped.

Daniel put the car in gear. "Are you done hiding yet? Because I am looking."

"Where are we going?"

"Back to your place."

"I thought you wanted to talk."

"I did, but if we keep sitting here talking I am going to kiss you, and right now I don't think either of us is ready for that. We just moved past the duck-joke phase." Nearly the same words he had used last time. Would they ever be ready?

thirty

CANDACE LET OUT A LOW whistle from where she stood scrambling eggs. "Jeans, girl? I can't remember the last time I saw you in a pair."

"Daniel asked if I would go on a walk with him this morning, and he said he thought jeans would be better than a skirt."

"You two didn't talk as long as I thought you would last night."

"Are you fishing for details?" Mandy poured herself a glass of milk.

"Definitely." Candace moved the pan off the element.

"Then answer me this. Was last night a setup?"

Candace's grin was answer enough. "One of the better ones I have ever tried, don't you think? Poor Colin, having to back the car up into a tree. He did most of the work. I only had to get you to the store at the right time. Spill."

"There isn't much to spill. We dropped off groceries, had ice cream with the two of you, and agreed to talk more today. He explained things that happened in New York. I shouldn't have paid so much attention to the tabloids. But you knew, didn't you."

Candace nodded. "Kissing?"

Mandy felt her face heat. "No kissing."

"You are blushing."

"What if I want to kiss him but I shouldn't? It isn't any fun being one of many. Even if I discount all his dates this year, there are still many others." Mandy finished her milk. "I just need to say good-bye."

"You realize he never looks at other women the way he does you? He is kind, but his eyes don't go all soft. You can see it in the photos."

They heard the truck in the driveway.

Candace tilted her head. "Should I be worried to send you out with him?"

Mandy grabbed a sweater. "No. I know what I am getting into this time."

Daniel opened the door for Mandy to get into the truck. "Too bad you are still not wearing the boot."

"What do you mean?" Mandy pulled on her seat belt.

"No excuse to hold you." Daniel shut the door.

Drat. If he talked like that all morning, she was going to have a hard time saying good-bye. "So, you never told me where we are going."

"Nope, it is a surprise. There are some clues in that folder on the dash." Daniel backed out of the drive.

Mandy opened the folder. "Who is Noah Crawford?"

"My great-grandfather. In case you didn't recognize it, Daniel Fowler is your great-grandfather."

"So your great-grandfather gave my great-grandfather ten acres of land and a house?"

"That is how I read it."

"Why?"

"Daniel Fowler saved Adam Crawford, Noah's brother, during one of the battles of World War I. Then, after the war, he brought Adam home. Adam suffered from shell shock, or what we call PTSD. Noah was impressed by Daniel Fowler's friendship and courage. In saving Adam, your great-grandfather lost his arm. Noah made him a manager of sorts over the farm and estate and gave him the land. I think there is more to the story. I have a researcher trying to find it, but Noah named his son Daniel. Technically as Daniel Noah Crawford the third, I am named for your great-grandfather."

"Weird." Mandy went back to reading. "I am terrible at legalese, but this says the property can never be sold."

"Nope."

"But my uncle—"

"Sold the house and land illegally and defrauded you of land that was yours. Your Grandma Mae put it in a trust for you since your father didn't want it, and your uncle only wanted to sell the property because of the natural gas. I'm kind of glad he did."

"What? Why?"

"Because if you had gotten the house, you would have been there the night of the tornado, and we both know the siren is hard to hear out here. You might not have woken up." Daniel turned onto a familiar road. "I know I don't deserve much of your trust, but will you close your eyes until I ask you to open them?"

Mandy closed her eyes. "Why are you driving back here?"

"Just a tiny bit of trust, please. I do drive better than Colin."

"Did he confess the crash was deliberate last night?" Mandy had a hard time keeping her eyes closed.

"Of course, that is why Colin is taking the car to a repair shop today." The truck slowed and turned. Gravel crunched under its tires as they came to a stop. "Stay right there and keep your eyes closed."

Daniel came and opened her door and reached across her to undo the seat belt. "Come on." He settled his hands on her waist and guided her down to the ground. His hands didn't move.

"What are you doing?" Mandy was surprised at how breathless her question came out.

"I am making faces to make sure your eyes are closed."

Mandy's chin lifted.

"No, keep them closed for another minute." His hands left

her waist and took hers. "Come on. Don't worry, I won't run you into anything."

The breeze tickled Mandy's nose, and she could smell wild flowers with a hint of lilac. "It smells like Grandma Mae's yard."

Daniel moved behind her and placed his hands on her shoulders, then leaned in close, his breath fanning her cheek. "Okay, Amanda, open your eyes."

It wasn't possible. The tornado had destroyed it. "Oh, Grandma Mae." Mandy wasn't sure if she'd said the words out loud or to herself as she took a step forward, half expecting the house to disappear. She reached the steps and tested them with her foot. "It is real. I don't understand."

"It is in the original contract—land and house. If ever the home needed repair, my great-grandfather would fix it. My grandfather did, and my father kept the bargain. Now it is my turn."

"But, Daniel, this is more than repair."

"I wasn't going to show the house to you until it was finished, but I thought you might want to deal with the interior decorating yourself. There are also a few updates, such as central air and the appliances. Come and see. When they excavated the old cellar, they found some brick from the chimney. I had them use the bricks in the restoration."

Mandy ran her hands over the fireplace, her mind screaming the question she didn't dare ask. Was this a good-bye or a hello? She walked through the dining room, where the wainscoting was already primed and the windows still had stickers on them. She knelt to touch the floor. Real hardwood. The built-in hutch stood empty. "Did I tell you I have all of Grandma Mae's china in storage?"

Daniel answered from the doorway, where he watched her. "No, you didn't."

"When I was little, I thought Grandma's house was huge, but then as I got older and saw other houses, I realized how small it was. But it feels bigger to me. Is it because there is no furniture?"

"This house has about a thousand more square feet than the

one you remember. The old cellar wouldn't support a new house, I had them enlarge the entire thing, The ceilings are higher to keep everything in proportion. Go see the rest."

Mandy wandered through the rooms and finally up the stairs to her old room. Daniel followed her. Mandy didn't care if he was smiling like the Cheshire cat. She went over to the window. "The trees are taller, but I can still see your old room."

"Really?" Daniel leaned against the doorframe.

Several scratches on the window frame drew her attention. She ran her fingers over them, recognizing the Morse code chart she had gotten into trouble for carving years ago.

Daniel came to stand behind her. His hand covered hers. "I thought you still might need the chart to remember all your letters."

"But why?" Why the code? Why this house? Why are you staring at me that way? Kiss me, please. No, don't.

"Because I still like Morse better than texting. Come on, we still have our hike." He grabbed her hand and tugged her from the room, down the stairs, and out of the back door. Past the old garden spot, a new white-pole fence gaped wide where one of the rails had been removed. Daniel lead her through the hole.

What happened to the chain link one? "You need to mend that." Mandy inspected the board lying on the ground for damage.

Daniel raised his brows. "I thought I did this morning when I moved those boards out of the way. Some fences work better this way."

Mandy looked at the hole. *Good fences make good neighbors but lousy lovers.* What did a newly built and deliberately broken fence make?

At the top of the hill, Mandy stopped and grabbed Daniel's arm. The mansion's windows gleamed in the sunshine. "You repaired the roof and the shutters. Did someone repaint the exterior too? How did I not notice?"

"Most of the work has been done on the sides that can't be seen from the road. Before the restoration can continue, I need your ideas on a couple of things." And I need you to stop looking at me like that. I have been trying not to kiss you ever since I picked you up. Do you know how amazing you look in jeans?" He tugged on her hand again and led them to the front door.

"I thought you said you didn't ever want to go in the mansion again. Isn't that why you stay in the caretaker's house?"

"Yes, but I have done a lot of thinking about that summer. Did you know you taught me to have fun? I don't think I ever laughed as much as I did that year. Do you remember playing hide-and-go-seek?"

"Getting caught in the dumbwaiter."

"Yes, that summer was difficult. My father marched me into my grandfather's office and told me Mother was dying, and I was left there with a man I hardly knew. The man always sat behind the desk. He told me to go play. Do you have any idea how boring it got playing video games all alone? Then you came through the broken fence." They walked into the office. "After I left your place last night, I came in here for the first time since I was nine. I didn't see my grandfather waving his hand at a servant to take me away. I saw you in pigtails, blowing a bubble and asking him if he had any books on Morse code while I hid in the hallway. Then I went in the kitchen, and you were there making cookies with our old cook. I went upstairs and stood at my old window, waiting for your flashlight to blink N-Y."

"I know this spring has probably been the worst of your life, starting with me scaring you into breaking your foot, then getting half of the women in New York to kiss me. I didn't kiss any of them back."

"What?" Mandy looked up from the dustcloth-covered chair she had been toying with.

"I didn't kiss any of them back. In fact, two of them I had to beg to show some affection in front of the cameras. Had I known I was going to get licked, I would have never done that."

Mandy took a step forward. "You had to ask Miss Long-Tongued-Really-Bad-Singer to lick you?"

"I asked for a kiss on the cheek."

"Why?"

"Because of Miss—"

Mandy held up her hand. "No, why didn't you tell me? I would have understood."

Daniel stepped around the desk and took her hand. "When our date hit the social media without the arrangements and nondisclosures, legal decided to not manipulate things. They didn't think they could trust you with the truth and get you to sign the papers. I also had signed papers, and I was reminded almost daily that I couldn't say a word to you. At first, when you started to ignore me, I thought it might be for the best."

"What changed your mind?"

"I got an apartment in Manhattan, and I came back to the most hideous pink-and-purple and orange-and-yellow furniture, and I couldn't laugh."

Mandy put her hand over her mouth. "Pink? Please tell me you have a photo."

Daniel handed her his phone. Mandy started to laugh.

"It gets worse." He flipped to the photo of the bear.

"No!" Mandy stopped laughing, her eyes wide, and she dashed out of the room.

It was Daniel's turn to laugh. He hoped she made it to the bathroom in time. He had thought she would have grown out of the need to run for a bathroom every time she laughed too hard.

"So, what did you want to show me?" Mandy decided not to reference her hasty exit. At least she didn't need to change her pants.

Daniel motioned for her to follow. "In the parlor—or is it "drawing room"? I never got all those names straight."

They entered a dark-paneled room where a dustcover hid a full grand. "I believe this is the music room."

On one side of the room, six easels were set up. "I need to know what you would have me do with the house."

"Me?"

Daniel only nodded.

Mandy pointed to the third one. "Please, not that."

"Agreed. The bordello is out. I also veto the private school. Too many snobs sending their children away."

"Agreed."

That left the family home, art museum, sanitarium, and country club.

"I don't know that I want to see golf balls in the duck pond. After all, I did promise not to hurt the pond. I don't know if they do mental health units that way or if we might find a buyer. I am not getting into health care—too many government regulations."

"Well, that brings us down to two."

"It is too big for a family home." Mandy's voice cracked as she said it.

"Probably right. But I think there is another option."

Mandy turned to face him.

Daniel gestured to the cleanest of the buildings. "This place would be a wonderful multi-purpose community building with a museum and community classrooms. The caretaker's house is much more suited to a family home, as is the back half of this house. Did you ever think of dividing it? Of course, your house would make a very nice family home."

What was he insinuating? Mandy needed more air. "No, I didn't think much of what was inside."

"You did on a couple of them. See? You put a crib in this window of the family home. And look what you put in the windows of this one."

"I'd rather not."

Daniel laughed. "You must have been very mad to create this one, judging by your blush. I still want to see the original."

When unicorns land on your lawn. Mandy backed up a step as the heat in her face grew. "I don't think you do."

Surprisingly, Daniel didn't advance. "It must have been very, very bad."

Mandy felt the blush to her toes.

Daniel moved on to a new subject. "We have time to decide. There are 630 acres here, and I have thought of several uses for some of the land."

Not sure what to do with the "we," she ignored it. "Aren't you selling?"

"I have thought of selling the north section that used to be the cornfields to the Amish. I hear they are looking for more land in the area. Maybe put the mansion in some sort of charitable trust." He looked at his watch. "I think it's time for lunch. Shall we go see what Hank's posterity has to say about that?" They left the house through the kitchen, where Daniel grabbed a picnic basket. Mandy was impressed. He hadn't had long to plan.

He entwined his fingers with hers, and they headed to the pond. As they drew near, the ducks started quacking.

"Do you hear what they are saying?" asked Daniel.

"Quack-quack-quack?"

"No, I hear 'quack-quack, quack-honk-quack-quack, honk-quack-honk-quack."

"I-L-C—I love cookies?" Mandy's heart sped up. She was pretty sure she knew what he was trying to say, but she needed to hear it.

"Oops, that last one should have been a honk for *Y*." Daniel set the basket down.

"The ducks love me?"

Daniel shook his head and settled his hands on her waist. "Not the ducks. Me." He stepped closer and started to lower his head, his eyes tracking hers, then lowering to her mouth.

Mandy stood on her tiptoes and did what every girl was dying to do. She kissed Daniel Crawford hello. Then she wrapped her arms around his neck and kissed him some more.

He kissed her back.

And while they embraced, Hank's great-grandson stuck his head in the basket and ran off with a sandwich.

Epilogue

CANDACE ADJUSTED MANDY'S VEIL. "THERE you go—something new. I still can't believe that dress is nearly seventy years old. Not many brides wear the groom's grandmother's dress."

"And the maid of honor too. I loved that pale-yellow dress from the time I was six. And I am glad they made duplicates for Araceli and Tessa."

Candace gave a little twirl. "I still think you should have worn this as you're going-away dress."

"Nope, this bride is wearing her dress when she leaves the building." Mandy slipped the garter with its traditional blue ribbon onto her leg.

Mandy's mother bustled in. "Oh, the ballroom is gorgeous, and it is fitting the first event at the Crawford Center be your wedding. I still think it is a shame you are not living here. Think of all the history."

Mandy kissed her mother's cheek. "Daniel and I will mostly live in Chicago, and we'll spend weekends at my cottage—I mean our cottage."

"Did he ever tell you where you were spending your honeymoon?" Candace asked, checking her perfectly normal sandy-blonde wig. She had explained earlier that she didn't want to stand out in the photos.

"Nope, but Terrance did let something slip about meeting me soon."

Candace squealed.

Tessa and Araceli came into the room carrying flowers. After being roommates for nearly four years, it was good to have them both here.

Tessa handed her a worn copy of *Wuthering Heights*. "Your something borrowed, although as much as this book has sat on the library table these past few months, I am not sure it shouldn't be yours. I'll never be able to read it again without thinking of you hogging Lover's Loft."

Mandy's mom wrapped the book in a swath of satin and lace. "There, dear. Everyone will assume you hold a little Bible with your flowers. Did I ever tell you the tradition is believed to be Irish?"

Mandy patted her mother's hand, hoping to stave off full-professor mode.

Araceli blinked and held up a hand to shade her eyes. "That is one wicked reflection off your cottage windows."

Mandy moved to the window.

"That isn't a reflection. It is Morse code."

"What does it say?"

Mandy studied the flashing light for a moment until the message started to repeat. "Same thing he wrote in the laundry room. Good fences make good neighbors but lousy lovers."

The End

acknowledgments

STARTING A NEW ADVENTURE IS almost as terrifying as it is exciting.

A special shout out to Ben Stowers, PA-C, who answered my questions about Mandy's injury and diagnosed the imaginary 'Lover's Fracture.'

Huge thanks to my beta readers and proof readers especially Nanette for her willingness to read things so many times. I would never make it through a day without Sally, and Cindy, whose advice keeps me going. Thanks to all the writers in Cache Valley League of Utah writers, and my Facebook groups, each of you has made me a better writer. Thank you for your part in my growth as a fledging writer.

Thanks also to Michele at Eschler Editing for the edits and finding oh so many little things to fix; any mistakes left in this book are not her fault. Nor are my excellent proofreaders to be blamed. Thank you ladies!

My family, for sharing their home with the fictional characters who often got fed better than they did. And my husband who encouraged me every crazy step of the way, and who is my example for every love story I dream up. The real one is better.

And to my Father in Heaven for putting these wonderful people, and any I may have forgotten to mention, in my life. I am grateful for every experience and blessing I have been granted.

about the author

LORIN GRACE WAS BORN IN Colorado and has been moving around the country ever since, living in eight states and several imaginary worlds. She graduated from Brigham Young University with a degree in Graphic Design.

Currently she lives in northern Utah with her husband, four children, and a dog who is insanely jealous of her laptop. When not writing Lorin enjoys creating graphics, visiting historical sites, museums, and reading.

Lorin is an active member of the League of Utah Writers and was awarded Honorable Mention in their 2016 creative writing contest short romance story category. Her debut novel, *Waking Lucy*, was awarded a 2017 Recommend Read award in the LUW Published book contest.

You can learn more about her, and sign up for her writers club at loringrace.com or at Facebook: LorinGraceWriter